SYSTEMA PARADOXA

ACCOUNTS OF CRYPTOZOOLOGICAL IMPORT

VOLUME 21
HIDDEN FURY
A TALE OF GOATMAN

AS ACCOUNTED BY BJORN HASSELER

NEOPARADOXA

Pennsville, NJ
2024

PUBLISHED BY
NeoParadoxa
A division of eSpec Books
PO Box 242
Pennsville, NJ 08070
www.especbooks.com

ISBN: 978-1-956463-53-8
ISBN (ebook): 978-1-956463-52-1

Interior Design: Danielle McPhail
www.sidhenadaire.com

Cover Art: Jason Whitley
Cover Design: Mike and Danielle McPhail, McP Digital Graphics
Interior Illustration: Jason Whitley

Copyediting: Greg Schauer and John L. French

Dedication

To everyone taking the next step
in your writing adventures— you can do it.

Chapter One

The case began on the radio as I drove into work. It's about a forty-minute drive from Manassas to Quantico, and I had the news station on so that I wouldn't die of boredom. Somebody was promising to fix Virginia 234 again, this time with overpasses. I yawned and reached for the channel buttons.

Then the murder reports started. A couple of people got shot in Southeast. Around here, that's known as Tuesday. On weekends, the body count is often higher. Somebody got hit in Northwest, which is less common. And somebody got killed in Prince George's County, Maryland. That was also not rare. PG bordered the District on the east.

I was expecting District Heights or Suitland next. Instead, after the commercial, the radio news explained a body had been found in Bowie, not yet identified, possibly killed with an axe. I made a mental note to google the incident when I got to the office.

We gathered around the conference table to start the day. Thomas Stratton is our Special Agent-In-Charge. "Strat" is clearly headed up into leadership. He's good people

They all are. It's rare to have a BAU agent who isn't a reasonably decent human being. Nobody cares that Kimura is Japanese or that I'm mixed race.

"We have a call from Prince George's County," he stated.

"Gang war?" Rogers asked.

"Holiday festivities shooting?" Carlson guessed. Cynicism kind of goes with our job. Charlie makes it an art form.

Stratton hesitated. That's how we knew it was a bad one.

"It's the axe murder in Bowie, isn't it?"

He looked at me in surprise. "Yeah, it is. How'd you know?"

"Radio news."

"You want it?"

I shrugged. It could share time with a dozen other cases I was consulting on. "Why'd they call us this quickly?"

"Decapitation, message left in blood... and they're already hearing rumors blaming it on Goatman."

"Who?"

"Goatman. The local urban legend. Half-goat, half-man, carries an axe, that sort of thing."

Carlson snickered. "Hey, Watson, we can move your desk down to the basement next to Scully."

A couple of the others laughed. Stratton didn't. Neither did Rogers.

Strat handed me the folder. I'd study it after the meeting and then give PG a call. Meanwhile, we had a laundry list of serial killers and sex traffickers to discuss.

Chapter Two

When I finally got to my desk, I read what they'd sent over. Twice. Then I abandoned my earlier plan to google it. Three hours later, I turned off Fletchertown Road onto Quintette Lane. This was the Q section. Except for Old Bowie along the railroad tracks, the city is alphabetized. The Q Section is west of Old Bowie. Almost everything else is south and east.

I hung a quick left into a small parking lot. A county cop motioned me to a stop.

I rolled down my window. "FBI."

"Yes, ma'am. You can park here. Paved path goes past a playground and then down over a hill to the lake. The gazebo's right there."

"Thank you, officer."

The lot had room for twenty or so cars, and my Bureau-issued SUV just about fit into one of the spaces. I counted eight patrol cars, a medical examiner's van, and what I assumed were unmarked cars. But no uniforms other than the officer on traffic duty. I got out, locked the doors, and studied the area.

Houses. Newish. An established neighborhood, the front-yard trees were grown. I didn't see anything unfinished. But there wasn't any obvious wear-and-tear, either. I made a note to look up when the Q section had gone in.

The ballfield to the right of the paved trail was a bit overgrown. It struck me as odd that no one used it regularly. The playground on the other side of the trail was in good shape, with recent scuffs in the dirt. I followed the trail around the outfield and then down a hill to a pond.

Brown water indicated this pond was not for swimming. It was a rough oval with a long, narrow inlet projecting to the northwest. The trail forked to meet another that appeared to circle the lake. The left fork went straight to a little gazebo at the edge of the water. From the number of cops gathered around, I gathered this was where the vic was discovered.

The cops were a mix of PG County and Bowie PD. As I came down the hill, I didn't notice any posturing or tension. Most of them stood a little way from the gazebo itself.

An officer from each department approached. From the stars on their uniforms, the two were chiefs. The county chief could have stepped off a recruiting poster. The Bowie chief was a little less crisp—somewhat heavier, more weathered, with a look in his eyes that told me he'd spent significant time as a patrol officer. That could go in a few different directions. I hoped it meant that he was a cop's cop.

The county chief studied me carefully through rimless eyeglasses. "Russell Williams."

"Aloysius Brown. Call me Al."

Not standing on rank confirmed my first impression. "I'm Tiffany Watson, from the FBI Behavioral Analysis Unit."

"Good to have you here. Well, no…" Brown corrected himself. "But you know what I mean."

"Yes, sir."

He waived me toward the pavilion and asked forensics to step back for a couple minutes.

I'd had no intention of entering the gazebo until they were finished. Plus, I could already smell the remains.

Caucasian male, nice clothes, white hair but not elderly, somewhat thin, and… a head shorter than he used to be. Not enough blood for a decapitation, especially since this one hadn't been one clean blow. No castoff, either—this was a dump site. The murder had been committed elsewhere. That alone justified their call to the FBI's Behavioral Analysis Unit.

The flip side of that was seriously unreasonable expectations, thanks to television shows like *Criminal Minds* and *Mindhunter*. No pressure…

"Any ID?"

"Not yet."

"It's officially up to the ME and forensics, but he wasn't killed here."

Both chiefs nodded.

"Any idea *why* he's here?"

The county chief's expression darkened. "There's a Fraternal Order of Police building in the woods on the other side of Fletchertown Road.

Follow the walking trail to the left, don't turn when it does, cross the road, and I think you'd just about hit it."

"So possibly a taunt."

I didn't miss the exchange of glances between the two chiefs. There was something else here.

"Do you see that box in the gazebo?"

"Yes."

"It's one of those Little Free Libraries. Forensics is done with the outside of it, although they'll need to examine each book page by page later. Why don't you take a look?"

I gloved up anyway. The Little Free Library was center-left, and the body (and head) were over on the right. Strat had mentioned a message left in blood. It was a simple double-headed arrow on the wooden deck of the gazebo. One side pointed at the body, the other at the library. The library box was painted gaudy colors—that was fairly standard for them—and had two shelves inside.

Both shelves were full. Every book stood upright with the title on the spine sticking out. I scanned the titles.

"Well, that's disturbing."

The top shelf started out on the left with spin-rack true-crime paperbacks. Zodiac, Son of Sam, that sort of thing. They moved on to John Douglas and Robert Ressler's books. They'd practically invented criminal profiling. The history's more complicated than that, of course, but the books' presence screamed, "Call the BAU!"

The lower shelf held a number of books about cults. Real subtle there, guy. (The possibility that the unsub was a woman was van-ishingly small. But if the body had been *in* the pond with the head still attached, I'd absolutely be thinking about a female offender.) Most of the books appeared sensationalistic, except for one that looked like a textbook. Interesting. Next to that was a manual from a roleplaying game. To the right of that were several local histories.

I winced. Local histories are fine in front of the fire on a rainy night. But the narrative tended to wander. Searching them for clues was going to be a pain in my butt, because my job was to figure out what message our suspect had sent and what else that told us about him. The first step would be forensics going over each book and building me a nice little bibliography along the way. Then I'd go online for duplicates of everything. I was *not* going to read three linear feet of books with gloves on. Forensics could page through them and send me pictures and page numbers of underlining, highlighting, or other defacing. Yes, I have strong opinions about not writing in books.

I stepped back and left the gazebo.

"That took time to set up," I told the chiefs. "It's definitely a message, but whether it's another taunt, an explanation, a cry for help, or straight-up misdirection... I don't know yet."

The PG chief nodded. "Darnedest thing I've ever seen. It would have taken less time to write us a letter explaining why he did it."

"You're not wrong." I shook my head. "Forensics will have to go over each book. Please have them compile a list of titles, authors, publishers, and editions, and add any distinctive marks from inside as they come to them. If the unsub left a confession, that'd be really helpful."

I switched subjects. "I hear there are already rumors. What are they?"

"Same rumors we always get around here. Urban legend, really," the Bowie chief clarified. "Goatman."

"Any particular reason for that?" I asked.

He shrugged and launched into the story. "It's nonsense. Every place has its creepy campfire story. This is ours. I'm not surprised it's already circulating, especially with the decapitation."

"How does everyone know about it already?" I tried to come across as curious rather than critical.

"Guy who found the body freaked out. Called 911 and ran back up the hill telling people to stay back. Within half an hour, tops, someone would have been ordering coffee and telling the whole Starbuck's about it."

I grimaced. That was... entirely plausible.

"Any chance he did it?"

Chief Brown shrugged. "He says no. Responding officers say no. The nearest doc-in-a-box says no. I've got an officer over there with him. He's pretty shaken up. If we're all wrong, he'll probably come apart and spontaneously confess in the next few days."

I didn't agree with the chief, but I didn't disagree, either. "I will say that stocking the Little Free Library does not seem to be the act of someone struggling to maintain control."

"Yeah, about that..." Chief Williams sounded like he was choosing his words carefully. "We don't get a lot of cold, calculating killers. Rather the opposite. You're the expert. It's why we called. The state of the body says rage, but the library says planning."

"Yeah. I can't argue with that."

He ticked off the possibilities. "Did he calm down? Did he set up the library ahead of time and then lose his cool? Or do we have more than one offender?"

The odds were against that last possibility, but to paraphrase Arthur Conan Doyle, we didn't yet have enough data for a theory.

"What kind of public statement do we put out?" Chief Brown wondered.

"I can't tell you if anyone else is at risk or not. Definite rage... but I really want COD from the autopsy." Because if the cause of death *wasn't* decapitation, the case was going to take a turn for the weirder.

As if on cue, Brown's phone warbled. He stepped away to take the call but was back within a minute.

"Patrol just stopped a suspicious individual. Kid ran from a routine patrol over on the Lanham-Severn Road. Get this: He's wearing some sort of leather collar around his neck."

"Kinky leather or US Marine leatherneck armor?" I asked.

He raised an eyebrow. "The second."

"That's... suspicious," Williams offered.

"Sure is. They're taking him into the station now."

CHAPTER THREE

I parked on the wrong side of the police station and had to walk at least halfway around the building before I could find a door that wasn't "exit only." I tried again and found the Bowie Police Department three-quarters of the way around: bathroom left, vending machine right, three officers at a glassed-in front desk with speakers set into the window.

Everyone who could squeeze into the observation room watched the interrogation. I passed up an invitation to be part of it. Not only do some perps crave having a federal agent there, but it's a bad idea to interrogate anyone without already knowing at least some of the answers.

The suspect sat up straight in his chair at a solid metal table. I didn't have the angle, but I suspected his shoulder blades weren't touching the backrest. Interesting.

One detective leaned forward, clearly going for intimidating. The other sat back at an angle to the table.

"Jeremiah Hawkins." The one leaning forward drew out the name. "You've got a record."

"Yeah."

The detective made a show of reading it.

"Small stuff. Drugs. Juvie. You've been clean since you got out."

I put him at twenty-three, plus or minus a couple years. African-American, short hair, long sleeves, jeans. I couldn't see his feet, but I expected functional shoes or boots. And a palm-wide leather neckpiece, tied off neatly in back with what looked like a shoelace threaded through holes at each corner.

"What have you been doing since then?"

"U.S. Marine. Should say that there."

"Shouldn't you be calling officers 'sir,' then, Marine?"

"Trick question." He paused. "Officer."

I did my absolute best to control my facial expressions, because the detective needed aloe after that burn. The pause before the respectful title had been the perfect length to convey the exact opposite.

"What's with the kinky collar, kid?"

"It's why Marines are called leathernecks. It stops edged weapons."

"Why? Are you worried about edged weapons?"

"The decapitation in Northridge Park."

"Why'd you run?"

"I had somewhere to be, and I didn't want to be out and unarmed any longer than I had to."

"No, smartass, why'd you run from us?"

"I didn't."

"Liar."

"Pensioner."

The kid never raised his voice, but he was on point with the comebacks.

"Listen, kid. We can put you away for a long time. One call to your command…"

I think he meant the threat to hang in the air, but the kid pounced.

"Call 'em." He rattled off the number. "Ask for Captain Creswell."

That's some self-assurance. C'mon, guys, cut the BS and get to what he knows.

"Where were you going?"

"To see a priest."

The two detectives opted to bluster a little more. I waited to see who would crack. It wasn't going to be the kid. He'd survived Marine drill instructors. No doubt he could sit at attention in a chair for the rest of the day. The observation room, however, would clear out long before that.

Eventually, the Bowie chief nodded to another officer, who knocked on the door and beckoned the two detectives out of the room. The chiefs, the two detectives, their lieutenant, and I ended up in a cramped conference room.

"Thoughts?" Chief Brown asked.

"He knows something," the detective who'd done most of the questioning stated. Chief Brown had introduced him as Winters.

"He wasn't on his way to visit a priest like he said." The other detective, LeClair, shook his head. "That's the worst story I've heard this year."

I didn't say anything because I didn't agree. I was pretty sure everything the Marine told us would turn out to be technically true. I was equally sure he'd left some things out.

So did the police. They held Hawkins, which they could probably do for forty-eight hours. They stepped up patrols, which was good. They started to canvas the area—also good. But nobody mentioned following up with the priest.

"What are you going to do, agent?" Winters asked.

All eyes turned toward me.

"First, I'm going to order duplicates of every book in the Little Free Library that Amazon has, while I can still get some of them delivered tomorrow. May I have them sent here?"

"Of course," Chief Brown told me.

"Second, I'll need to read the autopsy report as soon as it's available. Meanwhile, third, I'd like to tag along with whoever is going to question Hawkins' family."

A couple patrol officers from the Bowie force were going to conduct that interview. That didn't seem like the best option to me, but maybe they were really good at this. I couldn't call it a mistake any more than I could call the way the detectives had interviewed Hawkins a mistake. I *disagreed* with their approach, but that's just an approach. You always have the option to later say, "I had to come in hard on the first run. Nothing personal. This time, let's just talk."

I caught up to the officers as they were headed to their patrol car.

"Officers Dutch Yost and Omar Crosby?"

"Yeah." That was the tall white guy in his fifties. Dutch as in Pennsylvania Dutch, from that last name. The Bowie PD dated back only to 2006, so he didn't start out here. I wondered what his story was.

"What can we do for you, agent?" the slightly shorter and definitely younger black officer asked.

"Do you mind if I sit in on your interview with Corporal Hawkins' family?"

Crosby's expression said he clearly didn't mind at all, but he glanced at Yost. I'd already pegged him as the senior partner.

"Have you got some questions of your own for them?" Yost asked.

"I suspect mostly the same ones you do."

Yost shrugged. "Sure. You want to follow us?"

"Thanks."

The Hawkins family lived in Old Bowie. Brick house, gray shutters, chain-link fence, mown grass. Very neat except for the kids' toys in the yard.

Officer Yost knocked on the door. After a moment, it swung open, and a middle-aged African-American woman looked out at us.

"You here about Jeremiah? My husband's down at the station right now, getting him sprung."

"We have a few questions, ma'am," Officer Crosby began.

She tried to close the door, but Yost stuck his foot in the way.

"Ma'am, we really do need to ask you some questions."

"You can see my lawyer."

I decided it was time to speak up. "Mrs. Hawkins? What church do you attend?"

She looked at me suspiciously. "Why you wanna know that?"

"Just curious."

"First Baptist. Jeremiah was baptized there. All my boys were. Izzy. Jerry. Zeke."

"And Danny," I finished with her. I saw a flash of recognition in Officer Yost's eyes. Isaiah, Jeremiah, Ezekiel, and Daniel. Mr. and Mrs. Hawkins had taken their sons' names straight from the Old Testament, in order.

"That's right."

"Jeremiah very specifically said he was on his way to talk to a priest. Not a pastor. A priest. Why would that be?"

"He be goin' to warn Father Kelly, of course."

"I think we need to hear about this, Mrs. Hawkins. Might help Jeremiah."

"All right." She opened the door. "Let's go sit down."

From the family pictures in handmade wooden frames lining the front hall, I realized the toys in the yard probably belonged to Isaiah's kids. In the living room, hand-crocheted afghans were draped over the back of the sofa and several chairs. Mrs. Hawkins waved us to seats—Yost in an easy chair and Crosby and I on the sofa—and settled into what was clearly her regular chair, next to the end table with the Sudoku book, the remote control, and the bag of yarn for an afghan in progress.

Officer Crosby took the lead.

"Mrs. Hawkins, I'm Officer Omar Crosby. This is my partner Dutch Yost. And this is Supervisory Special Agent Tiffany Watson from the FBI."

Mrs. Hawkins gave Yost the sort of sharp look that said she didn't like him. She gave me the kind that promised questions later.

Then she began abruptly. "Father Kelly is old. He was here before, back in the '70s. *Mm-hmm.*"

I recognized the mannerism. It meant she considered what she'd just said important information.

"What happened in the '70s, ma'am?"

"That's the last time this whole thing happened."

"What happened back then?" Yost asked.

"Y'know." After a long pause, she spoke a single word, leaning closer and speaking softly. "Goatman."

"I've heard stories," Yost acknowledged. "But not from someone who was really there. Please, tell us what happened."

"I was just a little girl. So, I don't know all of it. It killed a dog, and people saw something that stood on two legs like a man but had a goat's head. It made a high-pitched scream. People saw it at night along country roads. One of the stories goes that a whole search party vanished—fourteen men. People say it was covered up." She stopped and peered at us over her reading glasses. "Now could the government do something like that?"

"Ma'am, this was the early '70s, right?" Officer Yost asked.

"Mm-hm."

"They couldn't even cover up Watergate. If whatever it was killed fourteen people, I think we'd all know about it."

"Maybe so. Maybe no. See, not everything makes the papers."

"Oh?"

Officer Yost sounded interested. I couldn't tell if he really was, or if he was just in professional-cop mode.

"There was a lot in Jeremiah's case that never came out at all. *Mm-hm.* In any town, there are people who know where the bodies are buried, so to speak, who don't say nothin'."

It wouldn't surprise me in the least if there were people in Jeremiah's past case who were involved up to their eyeballs and never prosecuted. Sometimes we just don't have enough evidence to satisfy the district attorney. State's attorney, here in Maryland.

"Does this have anything to do with Jeremiah's past case?" I asked.

"Only because y'all drew conclusions," Mrs. Hawkins answered. "Like my husband's no-good uncle. Come back from World War II not quite right. Always so mad about segregation. But not everything's about that. Finally went off and lived in a cabin in the woods and only turned up every so often to be a bad influence on my boys."

I desperately tried to avoid any more tangents. "Who would know about what happened with Goatman the first time?"

"Father Kelly, of course. Old Alice Crandall. She's always put on airs and used to make a big deal about writing in her diary. So, she might actually have her impressions from back then written down." Mrs. Hawkins looked at the two officers. "She won't show you, of course." Then she turned to me. "She might show you. I don't mean to pry—"

Oh, but she did. It happens to me a lot.

"—but you're black yourself." Her voice rose at the end, making it a question.

I didn't really want to have this conversation, but if it helped the case...

"I don't remember a time when I wasn't in the system," I told her. "I got adopted out when I was ten. Just in time, really. My parents always told me it was up to me what I put down on a form. I usually tried for 'All of the Above' unless I was going through a sassy phase. Then I'd be white on Monday, black on Tuesday, Asian on Wednesday, Hispanic on Thursday, and Native American on Friday." I shrugged. "When I joined the FBI, I volunteered for every new DNA test when it came out. Turns out my sassy junior high self was... pretty accurate."

"Don't say it that way to Alice. Play up the good schools you went to. I can tell you did."

Wow. There was still some rivalry between these ladies, all these years later.

"It sounds like you and Alice Crandall went to school together."

That drew a serious nod. "She was two years ahead of me at Eleanor Roosevelt, back when it was brand new."

"Thank you."

Yost and Crosby exchanged glances, and then Office Crosby stood. "Thank you very much, Mrs. Hawkins. I'm sure your husband will be home with the details soon."

She waggled a hand. "Maybe not 'soon,' but he'll be here."

Once outside, I turned to the officers. "Do you want to interview Father Kelly next?"

"I'm kinda curious," Yost allowed.

We turned onto Lanham-Severn Road (Maryland 564, if you prefer), crossed a bridge over the railroad tracks, and curved west. The Catholic church was right across from a little triangular Veterans Memorial Park that lay between 564 and a side road. It has a monument and a cannon. I'm not sure what kind. Not Revolutionary War or Civil War. Something more recent, maybe one of the world wars.

The old cemetery next to the church looks like the sort of place that could get a local legend attached to itself. I tentatively identified two of the buildings as the parsonage and the fellowship hall but I wasn't sure of the others. It took us a couple tries before we found a priest in one of the buildings.

"Excuse me, Father?" Officer Yost called.

The man at the desk gave us a startled look.

"May I help you, officer?"

"I think so. I'm Officer Yost. This is my partner, Officer Crosby. And this is Special Agent Tiffany Watson. We're looking for Father Kelly."

He smiled. "Father Kelly serves at Saint Edward the Confessor's in Bowie." Yost and Crosby nodded, and we were on our way.

I took a quick look around as I returned to my SUV. A sign identified the road at the narrow base of the triangular park as Zug Road. A cemetery, some woods, the Veterans Memorial. I could see how you could psych yourself out at night around here.

Then I followed the officers to Saint Edward's. We hunted around again before finding a white-haired man in a study.

"May I help you?"

"Officers Dutch Yost, Omar Crosby, and Special Agent Tiffany Watson, looking for Father Kelly."

"Oh! That's me. How can I help you?" He rose to his feet pretty swiftly for an older man. "Is someone hurt?"

The way he said it, I figured he meant, is someone dying and needs a priest?

"We're investigating a murder, Father."

Father Kelly froze. "Would that be the one in Northridge Park?"

"You seem pretty well informed, Father."

"At least four parishioners have brought it to my attention. They've called around, and a number of people are praying the rosary for the deceased. But, please, won't you sit down?"

Father Kelly pulled some chairs close. While he did that, I looked around. The room had plenty of bookshelves and some cushy chairs. A couple of the lower bookshelves held toys, kids' books, and games.

"This is your study but doubles as your counseling room?" I asked.

Father Kelly looked a little surprised. "Why, yes, it does."

Once we were all seated, he said, "Ask away."

"Do you know anything about the murder?" Officer Yost asked.

"Just what I was told over the phone, that a man was killed in the park. A couple of the calls said decapitated, but I don't know if that's true."

"It is."

Father Kelly shook his head. I'm pretty sure what he whispered to himself was the Lord's Prayer.

"Do you know Jeremiah Hawkins?"

"Yes. A promising young man. He fell in with a bad crowd but got away from that and joined the Marines."

"How do you know him?" Office Crosby asked. "You're obviously Catholic, and his mother said they attend First Baptist."

"We share a common interest in local history."

I saw both officers twigged to that statement. So, did I.

"That's very interesting, Father." Crosby seemed to choose his words with care. "There were some aspects of the crime scene that referenced local history."

Crosby did a masterful job underselling that.

"How did you and Jeremiah meet?" he asked next.

"Well, I guess you could say I'm at least partially responsible for his interest in local history. He was still mixed up with drugs. I almost said 'running with a gang,' except that makes it sound more formalized than I think it was. Anyway, several of us priests had gathered at the church on Lanham-Severn Road. When I came out, a group of youngsters, including Jeremiah, were vandalizing the cemetery, so I confronted them.

"A couple of them ran off, but Jeremiah stayed and listened to me talk about who was buried there. We got to talking about the history of Bowie."

"Father Kelly, are you missing any books? Especially any local histories?"

He blinked in surprise and rose from his chair. "Well, I don't know. Special agent, was it? Let's take a look."

I figured I might as well look at the bookshelves up close with him. He had quite a few religious books—a mix of textbooks, devotionals, canon law, and a smattering of other subjects. His local history section was extensive, but the books were solidly side-by-side with no obvious spaces between them.

"As far as I can tell, everything is here that should be."

"If you don't mind?"

Father Kelly stepped back. I scanned the titles and recognized two that had been in the Little Free Library.

"What are these two about?"

"Well, that first one is the dark side of local history, all stories about notorious crimes or allegedly supernatural events. It's a popular treatment, and the bibliography isn't as tight as a more academic treatment would be. The other one is anecdotes from the colonial era up through the 1980s." Father Kelly looked at me with a rather strange expression. "What caught your eye about these two?"

I shrugged.

"Why was Hawkins on his way here?" Crosby sounded impatient.

Father Kelly gave us a rueful smile. "I suppose he thought I needed someone to watch over me."

"Because you went outside to confront him, and he figured you might do the same if you heard something now?"

Great question from Officer Yost.

Father Kelly shrugged. From his eyes, he knew that I knew that he was copying my evasive answer a moment ago.

"But what's up with the leather strap? I get that he's a Marine—a leatherneck—but why wear it with civilian clothes?"

"To block any attempted decapitation." Father Kelly didn't add *duh* to his response, but I heard it anyway.

"Okay, Father," Officer Crosby began. "What we've got here is a decapitation in Northridge Park. The news reaches Jeremiah Hawkins, a Marine presumably home on leave, although we'll check that, and his reaction is to strap a piece of leather around his neck to avoid becoming the next victim, and then run—in long pants and long sleeves, no less—to you. Why?"

Father Kelly didn't immediately answer.

"Let me help," Office Crosby went on. "It's got something to do with local history, and his mother said you were here before, and it happened before, back in the early '70s. You need to tell us what's going on."

Father Kelly sighed. "You're right, of course. But I'm not sure you're going to believe me. It's Goatman."

Officer Crosby's smirk said he didn't believe him. Officer Yost probably didn't either, but his face was a mask.

"Would you tell us about Goatman, please?" I asked.

"You've never heard the stories? Well, he's half man, half goat. Makes a horrible screeching noise prowling around the woods. People say he kills couples in lovers' lanes. There are all sorts of different origin stories."

"I've heard them," Officer Crosby agreed.

"Not really something I've ever paid attention to before today," Officer Yost offered. "When did this all start? Had to be before Bowie got big."

"1957 is the first date I've found," Father Kelly answered. "Unless you count a Jesuit's drawing based on a story he heard from the Piscat-away."

"What do you think, Father?" I asked.

"I don't know. It seems unlikely there's some undiscovered creature right out there in this urban an area." He waved a hand in the direction of Old Bowie.

"Why did Mrs. Hawkins make a point of saying you were here when it happened before?"

Father Kelly raised an eyebrow. "Because I was. You know that priests get rotated, right?"

All three of us nodded.

"I was here in the early '70s, at the church on Lanham-Severn Road. Goatman was a big deal back then. Even bigger in the late '70s and '80s, I hear, but that's second-hand. Or third-hand. I was in other parishes by then."

Officer Yost ventured a question that surprised me. "Did you do anything about it back then, Father? Spiritually, I mean."

"Now that is a very interesting question, officer."

That was not a no. Officer Yost just waited. I made a mental note to ask the chief if he'd be up for sergeant soon.

Crosby fidgeted a bit, but Father Kelly broke first.

"Yes. I prayed."

"I know that, Father," Yost told him.

"If you are asking about exorcism, that sort of thing is very rarely done. I simply didn't have enough information to even contemplate it. By all accounts, this was a creature, not a demon."

We all heard the unspoken "but."

Father Kelly sighed. "I studied the situation. The stories, I mean. At first, there didn't seem to be anything to it. A rumor got started that I was looking into things, and I began receiving visits, letters, phone calls. All sorts of advice. While I can't fault their prayers or their willingness to help, very little of the advice was actually useful. It was, perhaps, what social media is like today."

Yost snorted, and I had to cough.

"A handful of the calls and letters were different. They were from people who, as far as I could tell, genuinely thought they'd seen Goatman. Whether they saw a large dog or a bear or perhaps even a goat in the woods, I can't say."

Father Kelly stopped speaking.

"Was there one more thing, Father?" I asked.

"May I be so bold as to ask you the state of your investigation in two or three days?"

Officer Crosby looked a little annoyed, but Yost simply shrugged. "You can ask. I don't know if we'll tell you anything—or even if there will be anything to tell."

That was only reasonable. But I was thinking about something else.

"Of course." Father Kelly turned to me. "And you, Special Agent?"

"I would be happy to speak with you in two or three days, Father." If curiosity didn't kill me first.

"That was interesting," Officer Yost said a few minutes later, once we were outside. "He knows something else but doesn't want to talk about it yet. Confessional?"

I frowned. "I thought of that, too. I hope not."

"We should probably check in at headquarters, see if the ME's got COD," he suggested.

"I'm guessing decapitation." Crosby's deadpan delivery was perfect for cop humor.

Back at the police station, Chief Brown updated us. "We don't have the official cause of death yet, but we do have an ID. The vic was Randolph Johnson Cartier III."

"Money?" Crosby asked.

"Lots. Cartier House?" Brown prompted.

"Oh, right."

"What's that?" I asked.

"The family were early settlers in the area. Their mansion is a museum now. It's just a few miles from here. But they've relocated into one of the nicer developments."

"What do they do?"

"Real estate development." The chief looked at the three of us. "You don't suppose?"

We exchanged glances.

I decided somebody had to say it. "That Goatman killed the guy who was turning his natural habitat into suburbia?"

"Isn't Cartier's son a developer, too?" Yost asked.

"Yes. And how many other developers are working in the area?" Brown asked. "Wonder if this has anything to do with the county permit scandal a few years ago…"

"Paperwork," Yost muttered.

I found some privacy and called Quantico.

"Strat? Watson."

"How's it looking?"

"Still waiting on COD, but definitely decapitated. Vic's a real estate developer named Cartier. Body dump was at a Little Free Library that was emptied and refilled to tell a story. I'm not sure what that is yet, but it included Douglas and Ressler's books, some stuff on cults and satanism, roleplaying games, and local histories. Locals have a guy in custody, Marine, twenty-three. All they've got on him is that this Protestant kid was running to tell a Catholic priest about the decapitation, and he was wearing a leather stock around his neck.

"Forensics sent me a bibliography of everything in the Little Free Library."

"What's the working relationship?"

"City and county chiefs were on-scene when I arrived. No friction. The two detectives who interviewed the Marine went at him hard and got nothing. I went with two patrol officers to interview his mother and the priest. They're pretty good."

"What's your gut reaction?"

"The mom and the priest seem to half-believe all the Goatman stuff."

I could visualize the funny expression Strat makes when he's processing information that doesn't compute.

"Get a hotel."

"On it."

"Stay in touch, too."

"Will do."

Strat hung up. He probably had a half-dozen files on his desk, each in its own sector, no overlapping, open space right in front for whichever one he wanted to pull toward him next, the same way he separated his food whenever we happened to eat out. Likely, some of those cases were more time-sensitive than mine.

Chapter Four

When I travel on a case, I usually stay at a hotel close to the police station. An officer at the front desk told me that was the Hampton Inn. Straight out to Maryland 197, second right, weave through a parking lot. Sounded easy enough. Plus, my phone could handle it if I couldn't.

The other thing I wanted was dinner. The police station was part of a city government complex next to an outdoor mall called Bowie Town Center. I'd asked the same officer for a restaurant recommendation, something open where people could talk to each other. He directed me to a local burger chain called Five Guys, toward the back of the mall complex.

I ordered a burger, fries, and soda, paid, and moved to the other end of the counter to wait for my food. While I was waiting, I filled the soda cup at one of those soda machines that let you play with the flavorings. I found the cream soda button and added orange. Orange creamsicle. Yum.

I'd tucked away my ID and wore a shoulder holster under my dress jacket, so I didn't look like a Fed. That was mostly good, because I was never going to get a table here that put my back to a wall. One of the downsides is it takes too long to draw. The other is guys trying to pick me up.

"Hey there." He was medium height, in shape, and wearing jeans and a T-shirt.

"Hi."

"What's a classy girl like you doing in a burger joint like this?"

Seriously? Has that ever, in your life, actually worked? "Getting dinner."

"You from around here?"

"No, I'm in town on business."

"Wanna get a drink?"

"No, thanks. I've still got a lot of work to do."

Someone yelled from behind the counter. "142!"

I collected my order and found an empty table. The guy had been a couple people behind me, so I had a few minutes to myself. It was a good burger, and they were generous with the fries. I drained my liquid creamsicle and went back to the machine for a Coke Zero with a full fruit basket of flavorings.

"144."

That was the guy who'd been hitting on me. I mentally nicknamed him "gross."

Of course, he dropped into a chair at an adjacent table. Regular (double) cheeseburger, large fries, large drink. I figured regular Coke, but I wasn't going to ask. He got a few bites in and turned to me.

"What kind of business are you in?"

"Consulting." True, as far as it went, but carefully phrased to deflect him toward wrong assumptions.

"I figured it had to be some sort of management. Not real work."

I get it. Some blue-collar workers don't think anything white-collar is actually work. It's not like there aren't attitudes in the other direction, too.

"Just remember to watch out for us working stiffs," he continued.

We really didn't need any more stiffs. Hopefully, this case, although weird, would be a one-and-done. But I'd waited too long to answer, and Gross had an expectant look on his face.

"I'm aiming for something fair and just," I said. "You know, for the stiffs." It pained me to add a smile.

Gross got distracted by a ruckus at the door, a group of girls, high-school age, chattering away. Racially diverse group, mix of clothing styles. I pegged them as middle to upper-middle class and went back to eating my dinner. Gross just stared.

They landed behind me and pulled a couple tables together. The girls were loud enough that I couldn't eavesdrop on anyone else. I kept half-listening as I thought about the case.

The locals would go through Cartier's life. You always check out the spouse first. I wondered how old she'd turn out to be, whether there were kids, and who stood to inherit. But he tied into local history, so maybe the display in the Little Free Library wasn't a complete misdirection.

True crime, profiling, cults, roleplaying games, and local history. Cults and roleplaying seemed like an easy way to shift blame. But then why bring up local history at all? It was apparently enough to send a Protestant juvenile delinquent-turned-Marine to a Catholic priest, who knew something he didn't want to bring up for two or three days.

Sherlock Holmes was correct. Watson still didn't have enough facts.

But I did realize there was a chance that Father Kelly was going to contact someone or do research or something that could bring him to the unsub's attention. I was reaching for my phone when I realized Gross was now involved in the girls' discussion. Worse, a couple of them sounded interested.

I broke in. "Excuse me, ladies. I'm here in Bowie on business, and I heard there was a murder this morning. I didn't think things like that—"

"Yeah, welcome to PG County," one of them told me.

Another, a slender, willowy girl, shuddered. "Well, murders happen, of course. But not like that. I heard somebody cut off his head."

"Ewwww!"

"Who was it?"

"Some suit," Gross answered. "Somebody who was kicked back at his computer during COVID while the rest of us took risks just going to work, trying to make a living, choking through a mask all day."

That drew at least one sniff. Gross was about one complaint short of breaking into the kind of country song I didn't like. I briefly considered him as a suspect. No, resentment over class and COVID restrictions simply didn't stand out. The chances that Gross had tried to insert himself into the investigation were virtually zero. He'd've had to spot me, follow us back to the police station, hang around until I came out, and walk in two people behind me. No, he was just Gross.

Still...

"That's an interesting theory, Mr...?"

"I'm not a mister. I work for a living. Name's Frank Yancey. You can call me Yance. You can have my number, too."

I rolled my eyes and pulled out my notebook. "Go ahead."

"You aren't going to put it in your phone?"

I smiled. "No."

But he gave me the number, and I copied it down. Just in case.

Then I turned around and looked at the girls. "Ladies, what have you heard about that murder?"

It got really quiet, then the willowy girl ventured, "People are saying it was Goatman."

"Tell me about Goatman, please."

She shrugged. "It's just a dumb story. 'Don't park with your boyfriend because Goatman will get you.' 'Don't go in the woods at night.'"

"The one about the guy's blood dripping on the roof of the car while his girlfriend was sitting inside terrified all night is pretty creepy," one of the other girls put in. She was black, or maybe 'two or more of the above' like me, average height, lots of braids, wearing a button-down shirt over a tank top and tight-leg jeans that ended a few inches above her ankles.

"I've heard that story before," I told her. "But it didn't have Goatman in it."

"I think everyone's heard a version of it," a short white girl said. "I used to live in California, and I heard it there. Bowie's version has Goatman, though."

"...mad scientist, though," one of the others chimed in. I had to play it back in my head before I realized she'd slaughtered the word 'obligatory.'

I went for confused. "Where's the mad scientist fit in?"

"Mixed his DNA with a goat's, turned into Goatman."

The girl with the braids shook her head. "That's not how DNA works at all."

"Ah, it's all crap," Frank Yancey put in. "C'mon, girls, le—"

I gave him a stern look and reached for my jacket pocket. "Yance, stay away from the minors."

"Hey! I do what..."

I flashed my badge. "What I tell you. Finish your burger and find something to go do, okay?"

"Is that real?" the willowy girl asked.

"Yes."

"Cool." Then she put it all together. "Are you seriously here about Goatman? So, you're like, what, Agent Scully?"

"You watch the classics," I observed. Might as well keep the banter going. Yancey sat there pouting. A few minutes later, he gulped down the last of his food and left without throwing his trash away.

"But you're investigating Goatman? For real?"

"No, I'm investigating a regular case, and Goatman kinda came up."

The California girl shrugged. "It's Bowie. Every time a dog goes missing, somebody says it was Goatman."

We chatted for a few more minutes before one of the girls pointed out they had to be going.

"It was really neat to meet you," the girl with the braids said. "Can I get your autograph?"

"If I can get yours."

A few minutes later, I had names and social media contact information for all of them. I almost certainly wouldn't need it, but...

Then I tossed my refuse in the trash and found the Hampton Inn. The hotel was blocky on the outside and nice inside. I got a room with no trouble and took my suitcase upstairs.

Each of us does keep a go bag. It's got clothes and everything else we need for a few days. On the first of the month, I swap out whatever's in mine to freshen it up. Creases set in when clothes are left in a bag for possibly months at a time.

I drew the curtains first, set up my work laptop, and then put away my clothes and toiletries. I had one email from forensics, the list of everything in the Little Free Library. And several policy emails from the FBI that I chose to ignore for now. I had an awesome job, but HR is HR anywhere you go. They're going to come up with a certain number of screwy policies no matter what.

It was about 7:30 PM, and I already debated changing into pajamas. But since the case felt a little too much like a horror movie, I sighed and opted for comfortable clothes from my go bag.

I opened the bibliography that forensics had sent, along with a tab to Amazon. I didn't order any of the true-crime books. We covered most of those cases in training, and I knew at least the basics about the rest. I already had Douglas and Ressler's books. I ordered the books on cults and the roleplaying manual. Amazon had some of the local histories, but not all. I already knew that Father Kelly had two of the others.

Then I started a search on Randolph Johnson Cartier III.

Over the next hour or so, I learned that the Cartiers went back to the early settlement of the area. Not all the way back, but fairly close. Randolph Johnson Cartier III was married to his third wife and had two children and several grandchildren. Wife number three was younger than the two children. To be honest, I didn't even blink. BAU cases make you more than a little jaded about stuff like that. A couple articles were worded in a way that made me think that the family, or some of it, had left Prince George's County for quite a while and then returned. I could check the online family tree sites later if it turned out I needed to know the details.

I figured another hour before I got sleepy, so I googled Goatman and found a surprising number of articles. After the third one, I started over, building a timeline and dropping points on a Google Maps layer. A good while later, I came up for air and assessed what I'd learned.

There was nothing there.

Goatman was just an urban legend. Sightings stretched from 1957 to 2007. The story was well-known in the area, but awfully thin. One of the girls at Five Guys had already pointed out how it drew on the slasher urban legend. It also incorporated sexually-motivated serial killers: Goatman supposedly attacked couples and dragged the woman off. Except that there were zero credible reports of this ever happening. There weren't even any non-credible reports, just hearsay claims. The intersection with the mad scientist genre was obvious, but the timeframe was too early for a scientist to be splicing DNA. Yeah, sure, mad genius ahead of his time. Whatever. The story gave his name as Fletcher and his assistant's as Lottsford. Fletchertown and Lottsford were two of the roads with Goatman sightings. Those names could be dismissed. The articles themselves said that Goatman's similarity to satyr and Pan myths fed the sexually-motivated part of the legend. Even the troll-under-the-bridge got dragged into it. Supposedly, Goatman hung out at Governor's Bridge or Crybaby Bridge. That sounded like a sighting at a local drinking spot. The articles explicitly identified Goatman as a cautionary tale associated with 1950s/1960s car culture.

The police knew all this. There was no way Father Kelly didn't know it. Or did our sources—I couldn't legitimately think of Jeremiah as a suspect—actually believe the legend?

The unsub certainly wanted everyone to believe Goatman was the killer. Or was it that he wanted us to believe he was Goatman? Whatever message the books in the Little Free Library were supposed to send bothered me. It's a murder. Call the BAU. Satanic. Roleplaying. Local history.

I shook my head. There was no indication this murder was associated with satanism. Roleplaying... what did that have to do with anything? Maybe just filler? The local histories, though... The most convincing lies contain some truth. Was it that simple? Sensational murder, call the BAU, here's some misdirection, and some history. Or was the history irrelevant, too?

That was a thought. I reached for my phone to see if anyone was still at the police station working the case and was shocked to see it was well after midnight. Oops.

Well, I could save that insight for the morning briefing. I made sure my electronics were charging, my pistol was within reach, and watched five minutes of funny cat videos. It was probably too late to save myself from a nightmare-fueled freak out, but still worth the try.

CHAPTER FIVE

When my alarm went off stupidly early in the morning, I couldn't remember any dreams at all. Go, silly cats.

I showered, dressed, collected my electronics, and headed for a breakfast place I'd spotted at the Town Center yesterday. I needed a little protein and something that wasn't coffee. They'd have enough of that at the station where they might as well be shipping it in by the tanker truck.

"Special Agent," one of the detectives greeted me. "We're working up Cartier's family. You want to read each one over and see if you spot something?"

"Sure." Not a bad use of a profiler.

The first dossier I received was Randolph Johnson Cartier III himself. Private sector, lots of boards and foundations, likely a major power broker at the local level, maybe even state. He'd have enemies. An anonymous source thought Randolph Johnson Carter III was an all-right guy for a CEO, but one really needed to keep an eye on his COO. I made a note to find out who that chief operations officer was.

Among those enemies was Estelle, wife number one. Blonde, attractive. She also came from old money, just not quite as much. It had not been an amicable divorce, focusing on who had cheated first.

They had two kids, Randolph Johnson Cartier IV and Cecilia Aileen Smithfield.

The son, known as either RJ or Four, had an expunged juvie record, a couple minor drug charges for which he'd spent a whole night behind bars, and an Ivy League degree where he'd been a frat boy. A lot of people seemed to think he'd been intent on proving those stereotypes accurate. Since then, he'd gone into the family business. Someone was quoted as saying he was a sharp operator but hadn't clarified in which sense.

Cecilia Aileen appeared to be a different story. Good grades. Not great, but good enough for a well-known private college. All the right extracurriculars and clubs. And a teaching degree, which she actually used. Married, two kids, taught locally. Got along really well with Daddy's wife number two. Of course, they weren't that far apart in age—sort of a big sister for her.

Two kids, homework to grade, and society balls? Cecilia had staff. I wrote down "interview the housekeeper."

Her husband was Nathan Smithfield. Upper-middle class, but not in the Cartiers' league. Magnet school, private but reasonable college, Senior Executive Service... I wondered how they'd met. All reports so far said happily married. That's the sort of thing you want to believe, but you have to try to verify it anyway—because we can all recite a list of cases where it turned out not to be true.

Their kids were preteens. Decent grades, no obvious problems. I supposed I could give them a second look if we ran out of suspects.

RJ and his family, though... wife Shawna, sorority, same school as RJ. Charges dropped... I shuffled dossiers. Yep, I had seen that date before. Same date that RJ had charges dropped. Drugs, alcohol, and a public fountain. Okay, so a little irresponsible in college is a long way from murder. A few traffic citations since then, all warnings.

I frowned. Who puts warnings in a file like this? I checked the days, then the times. Got it. All late evenings, which suggests she might have been on her way toward DUIs. Or possibly all the way there, if there'd been some influence thrown around.

Two kids. Randolph Johnson Cartier V went by "V," pronounced "vee," according to the file. And he was worse than a chip off the old block. Twenty, majoring in drugs rather than college, and not the comparatively less-dangerous party drugs his mom had favored. Oh, *and* a temper. Some incidents at school that sure looked like Daddy's lawyer got bullying reclassified as something else. Oh, and fires. It's never "just a couple small fires." It's one part of the McDonald Triad. The report had no information on the other two parts.

I let out a breath. The grandson needed a more thorough look.

The granddaughter was named Kailyn. Average grades, all the right extracurriculars, nothing to draw my attention. Another one I could circle back to.

The vic's second ex had been one Alicia Foster. Blonde, attractive... From the attached picture, she was clearly a "trophy wife." *Likes nice things,* the report read. Cecilia — the daughter — liked her. Divorced over "irreconcilable differences." Rumors maintained both sides had cheated, but none of that had come up in court. Interesting. Remarried to yet more money and still liked nice things. I shrugged. So what? As long as somebody's not breaking the law to get their nice things, what does it matter to me?

The third wife was Miranda Summersby. Blonde, attractive. Our vic certainly had a type. This one was British, with a trust fund. Prenups on both sides. Married fifteen years, the longest of the three. She was a year younger than his daughter Cecilia. According to re-ports — that is, gossip — they didn't like each other. Miranda had made some unfortunate statements. Not really controversial so much as just plain dumb. I shrugged. Sometimes people with money fall out of touch with the real world.

Obviously, we were going to want a copy of Randolph Johnson Cartier III's will. Who inherited what and whether anyone seemed surprised would tell us a great deal.

The conference room door opened, and I looked up. Officer Omar Crosby entered.

"You look like you're studying for finals," he said.

I smiled. "Yeah, pretty much. Interesting family. Anything new?"

"They just cut Jeremiah Hawkins loose."

I couldn't keep my eyes from widening. "They kept him overnight?"

Crosby shrugged. "Everyone wants the case solved."

Well, yeah. In fact, it was *such* an obvious statement...

"You mean people outside the department, too?" I wanted to make sure I understood.

"Yeah. Even a couple calls from Annapolis. Plus, the city's on edge."

The way Crosby said that told me that the pressure from people in the state government and the local fear were two different things.

"Do you like anyone in the family for it?"

I shrugged. "Too soon to say. I do want to come along with whoever is talking to them, though."

"That'll be Winters and LeClair."

From the flat pitch of his voice, I gathered that Crosby didn't approve. I wondered if he thought race played into it. But I thought it was more likely that the chief or the head of detectives was giving them another chance after yesterday's high-profile but unsuccessful run at their first suspect. On the other hand, I'd keep it in mind. A lot of times, if I just kept observing things, they eventually made themselves clear.

"They're planning to interview the last wife and the son this morning. And their lawyers." Officer Crosby sounded downright pissed off.

I nodded. Yes, the lawyers were going to keep the interview from being as helpful as it could be. No, there probably had never been any chance that someone like "Four" would forget to have a lawyer present.

"Do you know if they have plans to interview Cecilia Smithfield, the daughter?" I asked.

"Dunno. But why her next? She looks clean."

"That's why I want to talk with her first," I said. "Hang on a minute."

I made my way to the detectives' desks.

"Detective Winters? I understand you and Detective LeClair are interviewing Miranda Cartier and Randolph Johnson Cartier IV this morning."

"Yeah. Wanna come along?"

"Thank you, no. Would you mind if I interviewed Cecilia?"

Winters shrugged. "Knock yourself out. Long as you bring someone to take notes for the department."

"Absolutely."

I returned to the conference room. "Officer Crosby, would it upset the patrol patterns if you and Officer Yost came with me to interview Cecilia Smithfield? Or at least one of you?"

Crosby smiled. "They'll get over it. But do you know where she is?"

"Yes. She'll be at school by now."

Crosby gave me a look. "Her father was killed yesterday."

"Yes. I'm sure she stayed home yesterday, thinking about it all day. She'll think she's all cried out, at least for a while, and teachers would rather struggle through the day sick or hurt or grieving than write sub plans. Besides, it's her calling."

"How do you know that?"

"She teaches junior high. On purpose. She's got twelve years' experience. That's enough seniority to change grades or schools if she wanted to."

"You want to call ahead?"

"No. I want to casually show up, express our sympathies, and get a few routine questions out of the way. Then I'd like you and Officer Yost to step back, and Cecilia and I will have a girl-to-girl moment."

"That's, ah, ah..."

"Ruthless?" I asked. "I really do feel awful for her. But we need *someone's* read on the family, and I think we should start with the one that seems the most adjusted."

Crosby nodded. "Which school?"

I double-checked. "Benjamin Tasker Middle School."

"Oh. I'll go get Dutch. That's his school."

I pulled into the parking lot of the middle school right behind Officers Crosby and Yost. Yost got out quickly and did a slow three-sixty. I wasn't sure why, but I slid a hand inside my jacket.

"Sorry," Yost said. "This place bothers me."

"Schools?"

"No, just Tasker. I was on the PG force in '02 during the Beltway sniper attacks. Responded here when that kid was hit."

"Got it."

I knew the case. The physical evidence left in the woods nearby was pivotal. That's what Crosby had meant. Yost hadn't attended Tasker; he protected it.

"I switched over to Bowie when we got our own department in '06," Yost continued.

I nodded slowly. This was one of the cases, maybe *the* case, that had pushed Yost to the Bowie PD.

For all that he said he didn't like the place, Yost knew the office staff by name.

"We come by a lot," Crosby murmured to me. "Shoot hoops with the kids, whatever."

"We'd like to see Mrs. Smithfield," Yost said. "Do you have a resource teacher who could take her class for a little while?"

"Yes." The secretary's face clouded. "We tried to tell her to stay home today. But..."

A few minutes later, the three of us were seated in a small teachers' lounge with Cecilia Smithfield.

"Thank you for having one of the secretaries come and get me," she said. "I've got a TAG class right now, and if they saw officers come to the door, I'd be debunking wild theories the rest of the week."

Dutch Yost actually cracked a smile.

"I understand the police have to question everyone," she went on, "but... I'm sorry, ma'am, who are you again?"

"Supervisory Special Agent Tiffany Watson, FBI Behavioral Analysis Unit."

"Oh, of course." She gave me a watery smile. "I shouldn't even ask, but Watson?"

I smiled back. "I've been known to tell suspects they can talk to me, or they can talk to my smarter partner."

She laughed. "Oh, thank you! I needed that. Now, what do you want to know?"

"What we're looking for, ma'am..."

"Cecilia. Please."

"All right. Cecilia, we want to rule out everyone we can so we can focus on an actual suspect." I was shading the truth more than a little there. But she nodded. "We have to look at your family. It's not personal. It's just the percentages."

"I understand."

I saw that Officer Crosby had a pen poised over his notebook, and I was pretty sure Officer Yost's brain was set to "Record." Neither of them ventured a question, so I took the lead.

"How does your family get along?"

"We're a hot mess." Cecilia's quick answer was brutally frank. "I love them all, but we have our issues."

"Tell me about them, please. Where did you and Nathan meet?"

Cecilia Smithfield blushed. She tapped buttons on her phone and showed me a picture.

"My first year teaching. His father was sick, and his mother was taking care of him, so Nathan drove his little brother to school for a while. I had dismissal duty. We're not supposed to get involved with the students' families, of course, but he was so sweet. It was such a whirlwind. We were married within a year. My parents didn't exactly approve, but Nathan's such a hard worker they warmed up to him. And, well, they knew we wouldn't embarrass them."

"As opposed to, say, your brother and sister-in-law?"

Cecilia's face held the ghost of a smile. "There were some... incidents. Nathan and I... the parties are fun, but it's not our lifestyle."

"I understand you get along pretty well with your first stepmother."

Cecilia found another picture on her phone, of her and Alicia. "She's fifteen years older than I am, and she's always seemed like the big sister I never had. She never tried to take Mom's place."

"And Miranda?"

"Miranda and I have nothing in common with each other. No shared interests. We're only a year apart but I literally can't relate. It's very frustrating." It took her a moment to find a picture of them. They hadn't even managed to stand close together.

"Do you consider her a suspect?"

Cecilia's eyes bulged. "She wouldn't know how!"

That was an honest, unvarnished reaction, and Cecilia had just as much said that Miranda was too stupid to be able to murder her husband. Dang. I wanted to meet her now, in a clinical way, because Cecilia seemed such a nice person.

"What about the rest of your family?"

"No." Cecilia sounded positive. "RJ wouldn't kill Dad. If he got really, really mad, he'd maneuver with the business, not kill. It wouldn't occur to Shawna."

"And their kids?"

"They're teenagers!"

"Money? Rules?"

"RJ and Shawna make the rules, and they don't make all that many. As for money..." Cecilia held both hands palm up. "Their parents usually give them what they want, and if not, they'd hit up Dad or Mom. My mom and dad, I mean. The kids' grandparents."

"Anger?"

"Okay, RJ Junior *is* angry a lot of the time. But not at Dad. Just at life, I think."

"How is he with animals?"

"He's... not nice to them. Especially dogs. I don't approve, but at the same time, dogs don't like him, either, and I don't know if the chicken or the egg came first."

I didn't ask about Kailyn. Cecilia had a picture of RJ's family up. There was no way that a thirteen-year-old girl had decapitated anyone. I was more concerned she'd blow away in anything above a light breeze.

"Do their kids have romantic interests?"

"I don't know."

"Did your father have any enemies?"

"More like business rivals, I'd say. But..." She shuddered. "I can't see any of them doing this."

"We'd be happy to eliminate them as suspects." I ignored Crosby's faint frown. I'd apologize later for all the legwork I'd just volunteered him and Yost for.

Cecilia gave us several names. "I don't know the details. I just know Dad told us to stay away from them at parties."

"Fair enough. Thank you, Cecilia."

We stood and expressed our sympathies again. The two officers stepped back.

"How are you doing?" I asked. "Do you need a few minutes?"

"Yeah, just a few. I'll stop in the ladies' room."

"Is there anything else you want me to know?" I asked.

Cecilia actually stopped and thought before shaking her head. "Just arrest the guy, okay?"

I nodded.

Chapter Six

Back at the station, we compared notes with Winters and LeClair. RJ's list of his father's business enemies overlapped his sister's, but it wasn't an exact match. That was to be expected. I left the detectives and officers to divide up the names. Sometimes you don't want a Fed to be the first person someone talks to. Not when said Fed still doesn't have any real answers.

Besides, my books had started to arrive. I settled at the conference room table and began reading. By one in the afternoon, I'd skimmed one of the books on satanism and the occult. It was alarmist, poorly researched, and outright wrong on several points. As far as I could tell, it was also irrelevant to the case. It was time to break for lunch.

I ordered a burrito bowl and a soda at Chipotle and found a seat toward the center of the room. Nobody in earshot was discussing the murder, which wasn't all that surprising. I ate and thought, occasionally scribbling something down in my notebook for follow-up.

I'd just decided I could pretty much live on pico de gallo when I realized we didn't have much on the victim's movements. We'd looked at Jeremiah, we'd looked at Goatman, and we'd looked at the family. But I hadn't seen much on Cartier himself.

Or maybe I was just trying to get out of skimming another book on satanic cults.

I finished my burrito bowl, topped off my soda, and went back to the station. The timeline was up on the conference room wall. I compared times and googled locations. Then I added a question to my notebook: When did Miranda realize RJC was missing?

Then I went back to my reading. The next book had the same panicky tone. It even referenced the first one I'd read. A couple new twists, but after the "satanic panic" of the late 1980s, we wanted actual evidence. After wasting my time, I turned to the roleplaying manual.

When I caught myself thinking about rolling up a character, I moved along. There was nothing here, either. I mean, sure, there's usually an outcry against roleplaying games as part of a satanic panic, but—

I found Goatman.

Technically, it was a "beastman," but it had a goat's head, a man's body, and carried an axe. They were antagonist characters that a gamemaster might have the players encounter. Their origin story was fairly fuzzy: "unholy merger," "born from fury and dark magics," etc. Seeking revenge on humans, which they used to be.

I double-checked Forensics' bibliography. The unsub hadn't circled this section or anything like that. But it did seem like it was the whole point of including this book.

I finished flipping through the manual, found nothing else that seemed relevant, and then I thought about rage-motivated killers for a while. Rage-based left a wide range of possibilities.

Any evidence of sexual motivation?

So far, we'd been assuming no. Normally, those weren't the odds to play.

The conference room door swung open, and I looked up eagerly. Detective LeClair stood there.

"Autopsy's in, ma'am," he said. "COD was, ah, decapitation." He glanced at the books I had spread across the table. "Everyone's on their way."

"Thanks." I stood and started stacking books.

LeClair, Winters, their boss Lieutenant Atkins, Yost, and Crosby came close to filling the room. We could pack in about two more people before it'd start to get uncomfortable.

Lieutenant Atkins placed a folder on the table. "This is the autopsy report. I'll summarize the highlights and pass it around.

"Randolph Johnson Cartier III... died of exsanguination as a result of attempted decapitation. No defensive wounds. Hematoma indicates a blow to the back of the head which may well have become fatal in time. Victim was certainly unconscious after this blow. The ME counts at least sixteen axe blows to the neck and acknowledges the near-certainly that there were others he cannot reconstruct at this time. One of the early blows severed the carotid artery, and the victim bled to death."

Atkins looked up.

"What's the time of death, lieutenant?" I asked.

"Estimated between 10 PM and 1 AM based on body temperature. The victim was found around 6 AM."

"So, just five to eight hours for a *lot* of staging... Calculated... themed... no time to go to a store." I looked at the lieutenant. "Did any bookstores or libraries report break-ins?"

"No."

"Which means he either had these books already or could get them in the middle of the night. Some of those local histories are out of print." I paused. "Or he could have put the books in place before the murder."

"Transported the body, didn't leave much blood, wasn't seen, so far as we can tell."

"Made a second trip back to whatever vehicle he used for the books," I added. "Had to have everything in place not long after 5 AM. Have you found Cartier's car?"

The lieutenant didn't even blink at my sudden change of subject. "Yeah, at his office, and if there's a drop of blood in it, forensics hasn't found it yet."

"Was he working late?"

"Officially," Winters stated. "Unofficially, we suspect he was meeting someone. Too many lawyers present when we interviewed the widow and the son."

"I think the daughter's clean," Officer Yost stated.

Officer Crosby frowned. "She's a little too perfect."

"Let's go over where all of them were," Lieutenant Atkins suggested.

Their alibis were all pretty thin.

"Still think the daughter's clean?" Winters asked.

"Go call five random parents of kids in her classes and find out if they've gotten graded homework from two days ago handed back," I suggested.

Nobody took me up on it. They would when we really needed to confirm Cecilia's alibi. We tossed ideas around a while longer before the lieutenant held up a hand.

"What do we actually know about the killer?" he asked me.

"Male, killed the vic in a rage but apparently calmed down enough to stage the scene. Conversely, planned to stage the scene and lost control during the murder. No sexual component or motivation that we've seen. Well-off enough to have a vehicle to move the body and enough of a personal library to leave us a message of at least three hundred dollars in books. Fit enough to move the body. Manner of death suggests Cartier was the specific target."

"Will he kill again?"

"One murder isn't a serial. This one is certainly suggestive, and the BAU appreciates that you called us right away. But recent work with DNA and forensic genealogy has uncovered instances of one-and-done murders. It's at least possible that this one bothered the unsub enough that he won't kill again." I shrugged. "Five years ago, we would have all but ruled out a one-and-done. Now we at least have to acknowledge the possibility."

Lieutenant Atkins nodded. "Thanks. What are your plans tomorrow?"

"I need to read the local histories, and I know Father Kelly has two of them."

"Do you think he's involved?"

"He knows something. Or at least thinks he knows something," I answered. "I want to talk with him and with Jeremiah Hawkins, but not here."

The lieutenant grimaced, but nodded again. "What about the Cartiers?"

"Timelining each one to check their alibis should eliminate a bunch of them. It won't necessarily rule out a contract killing, but this doesn't feel like one." I grimaced in turn. "That's not very scientific of me."

"I know exactly what you mean," Atkins assured me. "We're looking at employees and competitors, too."

LeClair straightened up in his chair. "Employees. Contractors. Would any of them use axes?"

We talked that through for a few minutes.

"I suspect it's all saws these days," Atkins said. "But good idea, worth checking. Maybe an axe means something to someone on one of the construction crews."

Winters groaned. "Do you know how many people that is, boss? And they're day labor. Get picked up in the morning and paid at the end of the day. Won't be the same guys every day."

Atkins frowned. "I know. Find out what you can."

"Some of 'em are illegals, too. They won't want to talk."

"Yeah, grab a couple officers to help chase down whoever runs. Not Yost and Crosby. I want you two out asking questions yourselves."

Once tomorrow's plans were in place, I filled my briefcase with books and headed out, looking for a restaurant with booths where I could eat and read. I ordered a Renegade Sirloin and a salad at Longhorn Steakhouse and opted for the textbook on cults. The copyright date was over twenty years ago, and forensics had noted the copy in the Little Free Library had a price tag on the back from a Founder's Bookstore. I wondered if that was significant. Then I started reading.

By the time I'd demolished my salad, I'd skimmed the overview chapters that defined what a cult was. I started in on the chapters focused on specific cults just after my steak arrived. It was good.

So was the book. So far, I didn't see how it had anything to do with the case, but as an FBI agent in the Behavioral Analysis Unit, I was certainly familiar with some of the cults it covered. The text mostly focused on a theological angle, although it had some good behavioral observations. I started sketching a behavioral x-axis and a theological y-axis on my notepad and assigning values to different groups.

Well, this would be an interesting exercise later on, and possibly useful in future cases, but I still didn't see any connection to the Cartier murder. I skipped ahead to the section on satanic cults.

It was solid. Certainly not in favor of them, but not the-sky-is-falling alarmist. I made a note to look into the authors and see if they'd written anything else that might be helpful to the BAU. And these chapters repeated an observation I'd seen earlier in the book. People are drawn to cults when they feel powerless, and the cult offers them something. I wondered if that was why a copy of this book had been in the Little Free Library or if the whole satanic thing was misdirection. Pretty heavy-duty book for that, though.

Now that I was full of very good steak, I took myself back to the Hampton Inn and put on my pajamas. I was going to sit in bed and read the one local history that had arrived so far. It did not have an index, so I got up long enough to retrieve a notepad and pen.

The opening chapter's coverage of the Native American tribes who lived in what would become Maryland looked fairly spotty to me. I'm not an expert. Yes, I'm part Native American. We're not all the same. Or, they're not all the same. Since I don't follow the lifestyle and am not registered as a tribal member, I don't count. That's a lot of baggage for a teenager trying to bubble in school forms.

The next chapter was the Calverts and the *Ark* and the *Dove* and the initial settlement at St. Mary's. Then came the Revolutionary War, concentrating on the Howards, a couple counties to the northwest.

Aha! I found a Cartier in the postwar period although I'd have to check genealogy websites to confirm whether Pierre was actually related. He'd purchased a lot of land in the 1790s, which led to a falling out with the Native Americans (which ones?) over the provisions of a 1666 agreement.

I sighed and tossed the covers back. My laptop was over on the desk. It didn't take long at all to find out about the 1666 treaty between Maryland and a dozen Native tribes. It wasn't a treaty between equals. I went back to the bed, built a backrest of the many pillows, and pulled the blankets up to my waist.

Next was a chapter on the War of 1812, heavily focused on the British capture of Washington, DC, the attack on Fort McHenry, and the National Anthem. From there, the book went into a number of antebellum anecdotes. I noticed the subject of slavery was never far from the surface, but the book didn't address it directly. And I found another Cartier, a plantation owner.

And what was this? His son Pendleton Cartier had been a major player in trying to get all freedmen sent back to Africa. After that, he'd been equally outspoken defending slavery and then opposing the state constitution of 1864, which had ended slavery in Maryland. He hadn't gone as far as to actually fight for the Confederacy, although one of his sons had. That son died at Gettysburg, and Pendleton had reportedly sworn vengeance on the Union. Supposedly his ghost still stalked the plantation. Several deaths in the following years officially attributed to wild animals were said to have really been killed by the ghost of Pendleton Cartier.

This local history chronicled a whole lot of anger: Native Americans, slaves, the Civil War...

I read through the late 1800s and the early 1900s. There was a bit on the world wars, and then recent development. I saw Randolph Johnson Cartier's name a couple times. He hadn't been the major player in Bowie's development. It looked like his company might have been a distant second but crept steadily forward in the last forty years or so. I started to recognize certain neighborhoods, which told me I'd been at this for too long.

It was late. Well, I'd read as much as I could. Maybe my subconscious could do some organizing for me overnight and come up with an idea. I laid the book, the notepad, and the pen on the end table and turned off the light. I decided to chance it and skip the cat videos because that would involve getting out of bed again.

I jerked awake to my phone ringing. My eyes hadn't focused yet, and I struggled to accept the call.

"Special Agent Watson?"

"Speaking."

"I'm Angela Kramer, Prince George's County Public Safety Communications. The police chief asked me to call you."

"You have my full attention."

"There's another one."

I had a sinking feeling I already knew, but I had to ask. "Another what?"

"Decapitated body. They found it ten minutes ago at the racetrack."

"May I have the address?" My eyes were now working sufficiently to write it down. Some people can juggle a phone call and work Google Maps at the same time. Not me, not at 5:27 AM. I slid out of bed and crossed the room, solidly connecting with a desk leg.

"Ow!"

"Are you okay, ma'am?"

"Sorry. Just stubbed my toe."

"Sorry, ma'am."

"Not your fault." I typed while trying to ignore the pain. "Eleven minutes travel time. I think I can be there in twenty."

"Yes, ma'am. I'll let him know. Thank you, ma'am."

I didn't like how grateful she sounded that I was on the way.

I got ready in five minutes flat. stuffing my laptop, three of the books, and the notepad in my briefcase as I ran to my SUV.

I turned on the flashing lights but not the siren and followed a patrol car flying north on 197. We made it in nine minutes flat as the few commuters already on the road got out of our way.

All the flashing lights made it easy to find the scene. Especially the fire truck, which I'd definitely ask about. I approached the gathered officers at a brisk walk. We try not to run; it causes panic.

"Special Agent."

"Chief."

"We've got a second one. It's bad."

"An Angela Kramer called me and said it was another decapitation."

"Yeah. That's the least of it. I told all the officers and firefighters that none of the rest of this goes out on the radio at all."

I didn't really want to ask what was worse than a decapitated victim, but I did. Chief Brown simply beckoned me. I smelled it before we reached it. Fire. And death.

The body was in the middle of the track in a pool of blood that had already soaked into the dirt. The head lay a couple yards away. Male, Caucasian, old. This was *definitely* the murder scene. Ten yards away, two blackened timbers lay at an angle, one across the other. They were sodden. A tuft of fur was snagged on one of them.

"Oh, crap." I looked up at the chief. "Was this... a burning cross?"

"Yeah. A passing motorist called it in. Angela sent the fire department and everyone we had on duty. Fire's been out for maybe fifteen minutes. She asked the driver to come back here or into the station but he hasn't shown yet. Just so you know, there's a historically black university a little over a mile away."

"I understand." Well, in my own "all of the above" way, I guess. "Do you know who the victim is?"

"Yep. Wallet. Reynard Farnsworth. The family is big into horseracing."

Had I seen that name in one of the books?

"Is this their track?"

"No. Oh, I'm sure their horses used it, raced on it. But they don't own it. They do own a bunch of racehorses, though."

"Did the unsub leave us a library this time?"

"Just a burning cross. Agent Watson, what can you give me? There will be a shitstorm as soon as this gets out."

"Both victims are older white males. The killer may have a type, or that may be purely coincidental." I held up both hands, shoulder high. "I know, it's a blinding glimpse of the obvious. We need to check for ways Cartier and Farnsworth overlapped."

One of the Bowie officers stepped forward. "Uh, chief? I think I heard the families intermarried. I'm not sure."

"Chief, I found Cartiers in one of the local history books. One of them was a major slaveowner and had a son killed fighting for the

Confederacy. The burning cross is meant to invoke images of the Ku Klux Klan. And this close to that university... Either there's a connection to slavery and the Civil War, or the unsub is trying hard to create one."

Chief Brown let out a long breath. "Okay, I can see that. You mentioned possible misdirection the other day. What if it's all misdirection? Goatman, local history, the Civil War. What if he's just killing rich white guys?"

"Mission-based killer. Makes sense, especially with no overt sexual motivation. It's very possible, Chief." I wanted to be careful how I said this next part. "Honestly, there are going to be multiple possibilities, but that's a good one to check out. Especially any shared family history, beneficiaries..."

"Do you think this is financial?" Brown sounded a little incredulous.

"It's worth ruling out."

"Fair enough."

"Have you sent anyone to check on Jeremiah Hawkins or Father Kelly?"

"Yeah. I expect I'll get an earful, too, waking them up before dawn."

I smiled. "You might. But if Mrs. Hawkins has to go wake up Jeremiah..."

"Then he didn't do this one, and probably not the other one."

"Chief, one of the local histories that I couldn't order online was called *Bowiegian Tales*. I take it that's people who live in Bowie?"

"Yeah."

"Father Kelly has a copy. We can probably make the connection using genealogy sites, but if the Farnsworth and Cartier families intermarried, it might be in there, too."

"Once we're done here, by all means, go borrow it." Chief Brown turned to study the scene.

"Why didn't he move the body this time?" I wondered aloud. "He called attention to the scene instead. Closer to dawn, maybe, not enough time for full staging."

"Full staging?"

"The cross is certainly staging. Whether it speaks to motive or misdirection, I don't know yet. But it was meant to draw attention—and quickly."

"Dropping Cartier in the gazebo was, too," the chief stated.

"Yes. I've been wondering about that. Maybe he was killed somewhere that the killer didn't want us thinking about? Or simply too far away from the public to make a statement? Chief, could one of your officers check for callouts for small fires, especially anything that might be an arson?"

"Sure. But why?"

"Arson tells us a lot. If you find any, that could be the Cartier murder site."

He gave me a thoughtful nod. "I'll get someone on it. Anything else?"

I looked around. "Yes. Please have everyone turn off their flashing lights. You've got portables, right?"

"It'll be light by the time the ME and forensics get here and get set up. Not worth pulling portables out, but I'll definitely have everyone turn their squad car lights off."

"Keep all the officers you need but send the rest back on patrol. The unsub may be getting a lot of satisfaction over big clusters of officers. Especially if the motive really is just killing rich white guys."

Sometime around 8 AM, one of the forensics techs approached us.

"Chief? Agent? We've got something."

Chief Brown waited a moment, then ordered, "Spit it out."

"Hoofprints, sir."

"Right? It's a racetrack."

"Not like that, sir. You have to see this." The CSI sounded excited.

Brown shrugged and looked at me.

The tech led us to the body. "Right here, sir."

"Okay, that's a hoofprint," Brown agreed.

"And here."

"Also a hoofprint."

"It turned. It's not in line with the track anymore. And here, here, and here."

The chief swore. I didn't, because Strat has drummed it into us never to be surprised or unsettled in front of other law enforcement. But, yes, the hoofprints arced around and ended very close to the body. And they appeared to have shifted in place a good bit.

"Sir, ma'am, I think you should get a trainer out here as soon as we get a sheet over the body. Because it looks to me like there are only two hooves. Not four."

I have ridden a horse without breaking my neck. I did, however, end up with a dandy set of bruises, and what I know about tracking any animal would fit in a tweet with characters left over.

"How do you know the killer wasn't on horseback?"

Brown's question was very sensible. Mounted unsub chases Farnsworth down the track. Farnsworth veers to one side. Rider swerves, or whatever you call it when you do it with a horse, and whacks him with... the axe? I didn't like this at all.

"Chief, if we're proposing a mounted rider to go with the burning cross..."

"I hear you. I don't like it, either."

"Of course, the alternative is Goatman."

He snorted. "Some choice."

"Let me show you the books." I retrieved my briefcase from the SUV, being careful not to step on any of the evidence.

I showed him the roleplaying manual. "I think this one was included specifically for this picture here."

He peered at it. "Huh. Yeah, that pretty much matches all the stories. At this point, I almost hope it *is* Goatman."

Chapter Seven

I returned to the hotel mid-morning to shower and change clothes so I didn't smell like smoke. Then I checked in at the station and ran into Officer Yost on his way out.

"Agent Watson! Just who I need to see."

"Oh?" We stepped into the lobby.

"I've got a complaint from Mrs. Hawkins."

"That officers woke her up early this morning?"

"The whole family, in the middle of the night, according to her."

"Was Jeremiah there?"

"Answered the door himself."

I frowned. "Not great for establishing an alibi, but loud knock on the door pre-dawn, and he's a Marine. His body probably said 'sergeant' before his brain was actually working."

"I agree. Officer Brown said he was pretty sure he woke him up, though."

"Good. Have you heard about...?"

"Yeah. We need to solve this one fast."

"You're right. I'm going to call Father Kelly and borrow a couple of books. I'm thinking of talking to Jeremiah again, too."

"Do you want us along?"

"Up to—"

"Yost!" The shout came from behind the front desk. A sergeant waved him over. I went along.

"Dutch, I need you and Crosby to start checking on the new victim's family," the sergeant told him.

"Let me know if there's any crossover," I requested.

Father Kelly looked distressed. "I gather that is why an officer called on me before Prime this morning. Presumably, I was sufficiently incoherent that he concluded he had awakened me and that I had not just come from the scene of the crime."

I had to smile. "I apologize for that, Father. We had to check."

"Do you know who it is? The victim, I mean."

"The name hasn't been released yet, so please don't spread it around." I watched Father Kelly closely. "Reynard Farnsworth."

He shook his head. "I don't know who that is."

"Big in horseracing."

He frowned. "I know nothing about the subject. There's a track over on Race Track Road, of course."

I nodded.

"Father, I need your expertise on something. I'd have to share details that are being kept out of the press. Can you keep those private?"

Kelly just looked at me. "I'm a priest. I hear confessions. They have to be kept private."

"The victim was found at the racetrack near a burning cross."

Father Kelly froze. Time passed, maybe a minute. Then he spoke.

"This isn't what you think."

"Yeah, white male vic doesn't fit," I pointed out.

"It's not racially motivated. Not directly, anyway."

I waited.

"It's not race. It's not economic inequality. But they cause anger, and anger leads to wrath."

"I thought for a moment there you were going to say that anger leads to—"

"I know what you thought, and it's not entirely incorrect."

I was surprised Father Kelly had interrupted me, but then he seemed to straighten just a little before continuing. "It's not entirely correct, either, though, and I think we are going to need Jeremiah Hawkins for this discussion."

"I could go get him and be back in... fifteen minutes?"

"I would prefer we not talk here." Father Kelly's voice had regained its usual gentleness. 'In case it's being watched."

I held onto my special agent demeanor. "Watched? By whom? And why?"

"We'll get to that."

I frowned. "If we leave and pick up Jeremiah, wouldn't anyone watching simply follow us?"

"You may be right about picking up Jeremiah. We should meet him somewhere."

I pulled out my phone and notepad.

"Mrs. Hawkins? It's Special Agent Watson. May I speak with Jeremiah, please?"

"Why? So, you can arrest him again?"

"I have no reason to arrest Jeremiah. I'd like to ask him about something that he knows a lot about, not something that he did or didn't do."

"In public."

"That's fine with me. Where?"

I could hear them talking in the background, but not the actual words.

"Texas Roadhouse. It's at Annapolis Road and Highbridge."

"Thank you, Mrs. Hawkins. I'll meet him there."

I looked at Father Kelly with a rueful smile. "Texas Roadhouse?"

"That will work fine," he agreed.

It was lunchtime when Father Kelly and I entered the Texas Roadhouse, and the place was just about full. Jeremiah arrived a few minutes later.

The hostess shook her head. "Two I can do. Three? It'll be a while, unless you want to sit at the bar."

I looked at the others. Father Kelly shrugged.

"The bar is fine, ma'am," Jeremiah said.

Jeremiah and I took seats at one end of the bar, which gave us a pretty good view of the place. That put Father Kelly at right angles to us, so I could see both of them. As soon as we were seated, the bartender approached.

"Welcome to Texas Roadhouse! I'm Laura, and I'm going to be taking care of you today. Can I start you off with a drink?"

Laura was blonde, enthusiastic, and good at her job. Our coffee, Coke, and Diet Coke showed up in short order.

"What can I get you, my dears?" Laura asked us.

Jeremiah and Father Kelly exchanged looks.

"I got the check," I told Laura. "Gentlemen, go ahead."

Jeremiah ordered a ribeye steak. Father Kelly ordered a pulled pork dinner, and I ordered something called Road Kill. I wanted to see Strat's face when he got my receipts. Besides, chop steak, mushrooms, onions, and cheese — what's not to like?

I quietly filled Jeremiah in.

"A second man was murdered this morning. Reynard Farnsworth. He owns racehorses. He was found decapitated on the horseracing track, with a burning cross not far away. Don't share that, though, okay?"

"Yes, ma'am."

"One of the forensics guys found hoofprints. He suggests it's two hooves rather than four."

Jeremiah nodded, his face grim. "That fits. It almost had to be a Goatman."

I looked at Father Kelly. He was nodding.

"Seriously?"

"Yes, ma'am."

"You said 'a Goatman.' That implies there's more than one."

"I think it's a possibility," Father Kelly said.

Laura returned just then to refill our drinks.

"Looks like a serious conversation," she said.

Being evasive was never a good idea. In this case, it was better to be honest and be taken for ridiculous.

"It's about Goatman." I looked down as I said it.

"Oh, and that murder yesterday? I heard the police are actually looking for him. It. Whatever." She shook her head. "If you want to find Goatman, start at the Glenn Dale sanitarium."

"Why?"

"It's spooky as anything. Kids sneak in there all the time looking for ghosts and stuff."

"I think I saw something about a sighting there." In fact, I remembered it quite clearly. I was impressed the urban legend named a supposed police officer, just like it named teenagers in other encounters. But they'd turn out to be made up, just like the names of the scientist and his assistant.

"All sorts of supernatural sh — stuff probably happens there." Laura glanced at Father Kelly and flushed slightly.

Jeremiah was sitting there, not eating. "Why Glenn Dale?" he asked. "Sure, it's freaky, but it's not like it's Forest Haven."

"Oh, where all those kids died?"

I sat back and let Laura and Jeremiah carry the conversation. It lasted a couple minutes until Laura said she'd be right back. While she made a circuit of the bar refilling drinks, I asked Jeremiah for the short version.

"Forest Haven was a place for institutionalized children from DC. It's outside of Laurel, off 198 east of the Parkway. There's a mass grave of all the kids that died there. Neglect, abuse. It doesn't piss people off as much as it should."

"What happened at Forest Haven was tragic and criminal," Father Kelly stated. "But I do not think it has anything to do with Goatman. Think about it as a Marine, Jeremiah."

Now this was interesting.

"You're right," Jeremiah acknowledged. "Sorry, Father."

He sat there for a few minutes, pulling a pen he had clipped to the inside of his shirt collar and making notes on the paper napkin that had been under his Coke. At length, he looked up.

"I agree. Goatman is unlikely to be around Forest Haven."

"The floor is yours." I took a drink.

"First, ingress and egress. There are a limited number of ways in and out, and they're controlled. Okay, sure, you could hop the fence and get spotted by cars on 295 or 32. You'd also be operating more-or-less across the road from the NSA, and I'm guessing they'd notice."

I almost got Diet Coke up my nose. Yeah, they'd notice.

"Cross 295, and you're at Walmart. Head south, and you're in undeveloped land that goes all the way to the Agricultural Research Center and Bowie."

"That *is* where most of the Goatman sightings were," I pointed out. Then I started thinking like a profiler. "An organized offender doesn't hunt in his own neighborhood. But a disorganized offender might. Assuming it's valid to apply criminal profiling to something that's sup-posedly half-man, half-animal — which would require it to be morally, socially, and intelligently similar to people and to be committing crimes as opposed to hunting for dinner."

"What do the stories say?"

Father Kelly's question was obviously rhetorical. I saw Laura approaching and debated whether to answer in front of her.

"The Goatman stories say he preys on certain types of victims, and that means he's a preferential offender. That indicates intelligence and morality—or immorality, really."

"Sin," Father Kelly stated.

"Well, yes."

"Are you profiling Goatman?" Laura asked.

"Um, sure. Let's assume for the moment, despite the urban legend, that he's killing older white males. He'd have a type. It's not sexual. It's mission-based. He resents something or someone. It may be that specific victim, that type of person, or the victim may remind him of the person he truly wants to kill."

Laura's mouth dropped open. "Are you BAU?" she whispered.

"Yes."

"Cool! I watched all fifteen seasons of Criminal Minds."

Of course, she had. I gave her a brief smile, then asked a question. "Let's assume that Goatman—or an individual who wants us to think he's Goatman—is a mission-based offender. What would he want?"

Jeremiah gave me a grim sort of smile. "What the First Amendment calls 'a redress of grievances.'"

I nodded in approval. "But what grievances?"

"Double standards, people not keeping their word…"

"Perhaps the destruction of his natural habitat," Father Kelly contributed.

"Huh." Okay, they were both answering as if Goatman were real. But it was true that the expansion of Bowie had suburbanized a rural area. What had been plantations way back, and Native American ground before that.

"Oh! He's an injustice collector!" Laura exclaimed.

I smiled on the outside. Inside, I foresaw the conversation I was going to have with Strat. Yes, boss, I profiled an imaginary monster with a priest, a Marine, and a bartender.

"Does that mean everything Goatman's mad about might play into it?" Jeremiah asked.

I thought about unequal treaties and slavery and answered very cautiously. "Yes, but it's usually injustices particular to the unsub or perhaps his family and friends. History doesn't usually figure in. We usually classify those offenders as politically motivated, and I don't think that would apply to Goatman."

"What if it does and it doesn't?"

"Well, that's cryptic." I didn't miss the glance between Jeremiah and Father Kelly.

I caught Father Kelly's eye and nodded to Laura. He shrugged, which I took as "Go ahead. You're not going to be able to get rid of her anyway."

"All right, Laura. Can you keep the rest of this conversation private until the case goes to trial?"

"Sure!"

Evidently, Jeremiah had reached the same conclusion. "What if there's more than one?"

"More than one injustice?"

"More than one Goatman."

"Ohhhhh...!" Laura exclaimed. "There'd have to be, wouldn't there?"

"So, the grievances might change," Jeremiah continued.

"Okay, now we're proposing an entire homicidal species," I warned. "Aren't we jumping the shark just a little?"

"No," three voices chorused.

I looked at Father Kelly. "Jeremiah's mother said this happened back in the early '70s, and that you were here then."

"Yes."

"And you asked for a couple days before you told me something."

"Yes. I wanted to contact someone. I have not been able to reach this person."

"Where does he live?"

"I don't know. Somewhere isolated, though, so the old sanitarium is as a good place to start as any."

That seemed a really thin reason for starting there. I wondered if Father Kelly suspected his contact would be there. On the other hand, Jeremiah had initially tried to steer us away from the abandoned hospital.

Following Father Kelly's directions, we drove west on 450, crossed 197, and took the next major right on Glenn Dale Road. It wasn't hard to find. Trees gave way to a huge, mowed lawn on first one side and then on both. Brick buildings were visible from the road. One situated practically right next to the road had boarded-up doors and some smashed windows.

I pulled over to let what little traffic there was pass us. I practically coasted by, then picked up a little bit of speed.

"Where are we going?" Jeremiah asked.

Once we were past the old hospital, I found a place to pull off the road and began playing with Google Maps.

"Lieutenant with a map," Jeremiah muttered.

I laughed. "Yes. I want to get a sense of what else is around here. You know, just in case I end up running for my life on the grounds of a haunted sanitarium. And I see there's something called the WB&A Trail."

I followed it on the map. "Hm. Interesting… Straight down the trail, cut across here"—I showed them—"and you're on Fletchertown Road."

I put the SUV in drive. We found the WB&A Trail in less than a minute. It was paved. Then I turned onto Electric Avenue and cruised back the other way. The trees were too thick to see the hospital buildings. We came to the world's most awkward intersection. First, Bell Road arced back to our left at about a hundred and twenty degrees. It was in much rougher shape than the driveway not ten yards away from it. Less than ten yards beyond that there was what might be considered a four-way intersection, although it looked more like two roads casually sideswiped each other and continued on their way. Upon closer examination, the continuation of the road we were on was really the WB&A Trail. While it looked like the SUV would fit, it probably wasn't a good idea.

Just past the intersection on the left was a second driveway. Like the first, it led to a brick building. I saw cars at this one, then realized both buildings seemed to be private homes, not abandoned hospital buildings. I turned around and went the other way. We found a series of lane-and-a-half rural roads that emptied us out on Bell Station Road. I remembered hearing that name in connection with a Goatman sighting. Then we were at Cartier House. The sign said, "and Museum."

"Do you think it's open?" I asked.

"I'd rather not," Jeremiah said.

His reaction surprised me enough that I looked in the rearview mirror.

"My family's lived in this area a *long* time."

Oh!

I pulled into the parking lot anyway before turning around as much as I could to face Jeremiah.

"Right here?"

"You don't know what it's like." Jeremiah shook his head. "Sorry, ma'am. You might."

"No. I've got no idea. I'm 'all of the above,' but I don't know any of it. I never knew my birth parents. My adopted parents? Dad's Amerasian. Mom's Italian and Lebanese. They're great. Their daughter—my sister—looked at the results of one of the DNA tests I took and said, 'Eh, close enough, right?' But, no, I don't know what it's like. Sorry."

"That sucks, ma'am."

I managed a crooked smile. "If any of 'em went bad, I don't know about it."

"Funny you should mention that."

That was an invitation to follow up, so I gave him my best FBI agent's stern look.

"Jeremiah, what haven't you told me so far?"

He took a deep breath and let it out slowly. Father Kelly had also turned in his seat, and Jeremiah looked at him rather than me. Jeremiah opened his door.

"Some things are best said outside."

He climbed out of the SUV, and Father Kelly followed suit. I got out of the driver's side and joined them a short distance away.

Jeremiah did a three-sixty, evidently saw nothing that concerned him, and turned back to me.

"I don't know if your SUV is bugged. That's probably paranoid, but we can't take any chances." Another breath. "I thought I knew who Goatman was."

"You *thought* you knew?" I repeated.

"Yes, but he's dead."

Father Kelly spoke. "I thought I knew, too. But Jeremiah and I had different candidates in mind. I believe my contact is deceased as well."

"I figure you're carrying," Jeremiah said. "Do you have any other firearms in the SUV?"

"I'm not inclined to pass them out."

"Fine. You can carry them all. Just toss me one if it hits the fan."

Jeremiah reached inside his shirt and pulled out the leather stock. He tied it around his neck.

"I think it's time to call in our location," I said.

"*Your* location," Jeremiah corrected.

"All right." I called the station and let them know where I was.

It looked like we still had a couple hours of light.

"If we find Goatman, he'll probably be a hostile," Jeremiah said. "But as long as we're here, I have an idea where to start looking."

"Okay." I gestured for him to take the lead.

"You'll need your other weapons first, ma'am."

I sighed and popped the back of the SUV. Jeremiah didn't quite hover as he made sure I took not only the AR-15 but all the ammo. I also grabbed the Maglite. I slung the rifle and tried to figure out how to fit the magazines in my business suit.

"Ma'am, if we run into trouble, you're going to throw me the rifle, right? Why not give me the extra mags now? I'm not going to take any. It's 'I have no brass or ammo' every time we leave the range."

I handed him three of the four extra magazines.

Jeremiah led us toward the Cartier Mansion. According to the posted notice, museum hours were already over, and there were no cars around. The door was locked.

Jeremiah led us around the grounds. At one spot, he stopped and pointed. "The slave quarters were over there."

He didn't take us that way. We headed off into the woods instead. About a hundred yards in, I called a halt.

"Jeremiah! Stop. What are we doing?"

Jeremiah threw his head back and screeched.

I winced at the volume as the hair stood up on the back of my neck.

"Was that truly necessary?" Father Kelly asked the question mildly.

I noted that he half-turned away, maintaining polite contact but not concerned at all about Jeremiah. He focused on the woods.

Jeremiah gave another shrill screech. I winced again. That noise was really disturbing. It wasn't something I expected to come out of a human.

I reached for my service weapon. "Are you Goatman?"

"No, ma'am. That's why I enlisted in the Marine Corps. I wanted to make sure I wasn't."

"I think you'd better explain that."

Father Kelly spoke up instead. "I imagine you have looked up the various Goatman sightings."

"Yes. 1957-2007. And possibly something in 1666. Most of them are flimsy. There are allegations that Goatman kills, but none of the deaths in the stories can be verified. If a creature killed fourteen people in the

1960s, teams would have swept the woods until they found whoever or whatever it was."

"I concur that Goatman did not kill anyone between 1957 and 2007," Father Kelly said.

"For there to be an actual Goatman, either it would have to be a long-lived creature or there would have to be a sustainable population," I pointed out.

"Well-reasoned. But what if there is a third option?"

"Father, it's almost sunset. Is this the right time and place for formal debate?" I asked.

"What if—?"

A bloodcurdling screech sounded in the distance.

I jumped. The rifle sling was off my shoulder as I landed. The lengthening shadows reduced how far I could see into the woods.

"I think it came from west of here." Jeremiah's tone was conversational, and I reminded myself he was a Marine. "Ma'am, how much do you train with that rifle?"

I was decent but probably not as good as a Marine. I handed it over and drew my Glock.

"We should track him down before he kills again," Jeremiah continued.

"You're not wrong," I muttered. "You said west of here. That's over by Glenn Dale Hospital, isn't it?"

"Yes, ma'am."

"Father Kelly?"

"He needs to be stopped."

"Let's get back in the SUV and drive over there," I directed. "I'm not sure we can call in a freaky howl just yet."

We drove back to Glenn Dale Hospital where I weighed parking out of sight (which meant around the next corner in the WB&A Trail parking lot) against being able to get to the SUV quickly. Quickly won.

We were partway to the main building when another screech echoed across the grounds. Jeremiah immediately cupped his hands and returned it.

"How did you learn to do that?"

"My great uncle."

"Would that be the same man your mother described as your father's no-good uncle?"

Jeremiah laughed. "It would. Great Uncle Josh."

"And why did he know how to screech like Goatman?"

"Uncle Josh served in World War II. He knew how to keep his mouth shut. A lot of those men took stories to the grave that I wish we knew."

"I'm an FBI agent, so I know all about keeping my mouth shut, but I agree with you."

"He taught me how to do it and told me that if I was ever in trouble in the woods around Bowie, to screech like that."

I frowned. "Was he trying to get you killed? Or did he think Goatman would come and help?"

"The second. See, I thought he might have been Goatman. But he died years ago."

"And I thought one of the people who called me back in the '70s might be Goatman," Father Kelly put in. "He knew too much about the incidents. He came to confession a few times. We mostly talked about St. Ignatius of Loyola's book *Spiritual Exercises*."

Great. So, this did involve the seal of the confessional. And—

A screech cut through the gathering dusk.

"West of here." Jeremiah's assessment was matter-of-fact. "I recommend we not go into the woods after him. Or meet him on open ground. Let him come to us. Straight down the road is twelve o'clock, so we're looking at nine o'clock right now. Do you have enough gas to let the engine idle?"

"Yes." I weighed our options. *Why, yes, Strat, I handed the keys to an FBI vehicle to a priest so I'd be ready to shoot...*

Another horrible screech sounded. I probably jumped, but all I remember is thinking it was definitely closer than before. We'd parked a little ways north of the building that was right next to the road. Another sanitarium building lay off to our left, set further back. I could see at least three more buildings across the mown lawn. We should be able to see anyone at least a—

"Ten o'clock, moving fast!" The AR-15 snapped up to Jeremiah's shoulder. "Identify yourself!"

The dark-furred bipedal thing threw its head back and screeched. Jeremiah did the same.

I threw my keys to Father Kelly. "Get in! Call 911!"

The creature ate up distance with a loping stride and was already halfway to us. It had the head of a goat, and it was huge. But I was more concerned with the axe it carried.

My Glock came up. "Halt! FBI! Stop or I'll shoot!"

It went for Jeremiah.

He opened fire. Each shot from the AR-15 sounded like a metallic snap. My Glock was louder. I know I missed some.

Goatman clawed at his upper chest and charged even faster. The axe swung in a great overhand blow.

Jeremiah blocked the haft with the AR-15. Goatman had at least a foot and a half on him. It reared back with the axe, and quick as lightning Jeremiah brought the AR back up and emptied the magazine at Goatman's throat. I saw some rounds strike before Jeremiah dove to avoid the next blow.

I shot Goatman. A lot. Ejected the mag, grabbed the next.

Goatman was on me in a single bound. I ducked as he swung. I smashed into the ground shoulder-first because I wasn't going to give up the mag.

I started to scramble to my feet. Goatman plowed into me. The axe was gone, but a backhand launched me into the side of the SUV.

This time I lost the mag. I spotted it, reached—

Goatman's hoof slammed down on it.

I reached for my last pistol magazine.

A hoof threw me against the SUV again. Goatman kicked like a mu—goat.

Jeremiah opened fire. I could *see* 5.56 rounds hitting Goatman. He whirled and lunged. Claws scrabbled for Jeremiah's neck and slid across the leather stock.

Another bloodcurdling screech rent the night. It wasn't Goatman or Jeremiah.

I whirled around and gasped. A *second* Goatman bounded across the road at us.

"Jeremiah!" I shouted.

He parried the first Goatman's blow with the rifle.

I finally slammed the fresh magazine home and leveled my Glock.

The second Goatman tackled the first one.

They rolled across the lawn, biting and clawing. You've heard the expression to see fur fly? It's a real thing.

Jeremiah hurried to my side. "Can you stand?"

I struggled to my feet. "Yeah."

Goatman #2 was smaller. He didn't have an axe. But he wasn't bleeding from a couple dozen bullet wounds, either. When Goatman

#1's jaws clamped down on his arm, Goatman #2 slashed at him and then started pounding him in the face.

Goatman #1 snapped his jaws at him.

As soon as he'd let go, Goatman #2 regained his feet... hooves. I think that was his goal the whole time.

#1 screamed and charged, and #2 lashed out with a hoof. It looked like the goat version of a karate kick, and Goatman #1 folded over it. He went down, rolled, scrambled, and came back up. Then he grabbed the axe and bounded away. He weaved from side to side and fell to the ground once before regaining his feet... hooves.

Jeremiah tried for a shot with the AR-15, but Goatman #2 stood and turned toward us. He held up one clawed hand and made a soft screeching sound.

I tentatively decided not to shoot him.

Goatman #2 reached into a pouch he wore on a shoulder strap. Showing a surprising amount of dexterity, he extracted something small and white.

Yes, Goatman handed me his card.

I decided I was concussed from being slammed into the SUV.

Then Goatman pointed at Jeremiah's rifle and waggled one long claw. With a cheery wave, he turned and loped away.

I looked at Jeremiah. "What the hell just happened?"

He safetied the AR-15 before lowering it and shaking his head. "What the actual—?"

The SUV door opened, and we both whirled around.

Father Kelly emerged, hands carefully in the air. "I have the police on my phone."

"Please."

He handed me a cell phone already set to speaker.

"FBI Special Agent Tiffany Watson."

"Agent Watson, we have several reports of gunfire at the Glenn Dale Hospital."

"Yeah. That was us."

"Caller said it sounded like Iraq. Like a hundred rounds. Are you okay?"

My math was broken. "That... sounds about right. I might be concussed. Tell responding units to hold their fire. There are two Goatmen out here. One of them is friendly, and the other definitely isn't."

"Is anyone else hurt?"

Jeremiah shook his head.

"Mostly the bad Goatman. Listen, I need forensics, spotlights, dogs, and a helicopter."

"Is anyone with you?"

I handed the phone to Jeremiah.

"Corporal Jeremiah Hawkins, United States Marine Corps, ma'am. One hostile fled, badly wounded."

The next thing I knew, Father Kelly was helping me up off the ground.

"Easy there, Agent Watson," he said.

"What just happened?"

"My guess is your adrenaline wore off, and your body just figured out you were hit by a car."

"Reasonable," I muttered. I stood.

"I think you should stay there," Father Kelly told me.

I heard sirens in the distance. Nope, I was going to meet them standing up. Well, okay, maybe leaning against my SUV.

The first patrol car rolled up. Both officers piled out, shotguns in hand.

Jeremiah had already placed the AR-15 and my Glock on the hood of the SUV with the magazines in a row next to each weapon. Mostly empty magazines, I noted. Yeah, a hundred rounds might be about right.

"Freeze!"

"FBI!" I shouted back.

CHAPTER EIGHT

I had the same conversation at least five times, with the responding officers, back at the station, on the phone with Strat, with Yost and Crosby the next morning, and with Laura at Texas Roadhouse later on. I'm not going to detail all of them, because most of them went about the same way. The officers didn't believe me when I said Goatman had attacked us, but they knew we hadn't fired a hundred rounds at nothing. The water-cooler gossip tended in the direction of perp-with-a-mask.

Just for the record, a rubber Halloween mask wouldn't have done much about the magazine that Jeremiah unloaded into Goatman's throat.

"That's... are you sure those rounds hit?" Strat asked me. We were on video chat, and I could tell I'd worried him.

"I saw blood spray. I think we nearly killed him. I wouldn't be surprised if he bled out."

"Are you all right?"

"They made me go to the ER," I said. "Yes, I've got some bruises and a second-degree minus concussion, but mostly I've got a ridiculous dry cleaner bill."

I got the bark of laughter from Strat I was looking for.

"And I promise I'll eat my painkillers like a good little agent."

"I get it. You have to be tougher than the cops. How are the others?"

"Jeremiah Hawkins has a few bruises, but he's a Marine, so he's eating painkillers, too. Father Kelly was smart enough to stay in the SUV and call 911."

The video froze for just a second before Strat's next question came through.

"What's your take on the second guy?"

I'd been thinking about that all night. On the way to the hospital, sitting at the ER, driving back to the station again. Before, during, and after the three hours of sleep I'd gotten.

"I think the first one is the killer, and the second one has been trying to stop him and staged the first scene. I think the Goatman #1 did the second scene himself."

"I don't see how they could really be Goatmen," Strat stated. "That nobody noticed an entire species all this time, that there could be a surviving population... no, it's something else."

I took a deep breath. "I had an idea in the shower this morning."

Strat perked up. He *never* made wisecracks about me in the shower. He just accepted that was where inspiration usually struck.

"Go ahead."

"You're right. There would have to be Goatwomen. Eventually, a Goatkid would get spotted or do something stupid. But what if Goatmen are werecreatures?"

Strat's eyes just about crossed. "Wait. You're positing the existence of *weregoats*?"

"Yeah. I'm not claiming they have to be weregoats. Just that it explains the evidence."

"That's not going in your official report."

"Understood, sir." I really did understand. It wouldn't go in my *official* report.

"How's the search going?"

"Nothing so far. They're still at it."

Late in the afternoon, a call came in.

Chief Brown called me personally. "They've got a body."

"Goatman? Or an old white male?"

"No. Young white male, shot to ribbons."

I waited for the explanation of why this was part of the same case.

"Looks like he took several in the throat. Which is interesting, seeing as how you and Hawkins both report that he emptied a mag into Goatman's throat. Except this is a kid."

"Goatman was tall," I reminded the chief. "Jeremiah was aiming upward."

"Tell me you two didn't shoot a kid."

"We already told you that. Goatman #1 should have a lot of 5.56 in the throat and 9 mm in the torso."

"I think you better get over here. Where are you?"

"Out back of the Cartier Mansion in grid 67," I answered.

"You're close. It's north of you along the WB&A Trail. You can park at the Splash Park. Take a left at the entrance and go all the way to the end of the parking lot. There's a connecting trail."

"Thanks."

I checked out from my search team, found my way back to the parking lot, checked out with the search coordinator there, and drove up 193 and through the Splash Park lot as instructed. It was easy enough to spot the patrol cars and ambulance. The scene wasn't far down the trail at all.

If this was Goatman #1, he'd made it a lot further than I would have guessed.

I was able to pick out the chief in the middle of a group of officers. Somebody noticed me. I saw heads turn, including his, and he gave me a hard look.

I approached in the "standard FBI gait" I'd learned from Strat. The body was covered with a sheet.

"Teen or twenty," he spat. "No clothes. Shot all to hell."

He gave an officer a curt nod, and the officer pulled back the sheet.

"Do you have an ID?" I asked.

"Not yet."

They should. I did. Okay, not officially, but I knew who it was. Vee. Randolph Johnson Cartier the Fifth. The angry grandson.

"'Born of fury and dark magics,'" I muttered.

"What?" Brown asked.

"'Born of fury and dark magics.' It's in one of the roleplaying manuals left at the first body dump."

"There's no way this kid staged that," the chief said.

"Of course not. It'll turn out that Goatman #2 did the staging there," I told him. "They're all mad. Not insane but enraged. Pendleton Cartier in the Civil War, Mr. Hawkins's Uncle Josh, Father Kelly's source, Vee." I looked up at Chief Brown. "He *told* us how it happens."

"Hold on," he ordered. "This is Vee? Randolph Johnson Cartier V?"

"Pretty sure. Get DNA. And run it against his family — and the fur from Goatman last night. And the fur snagged on the cross."

"Fur?" an officer asked. He pointed, and I noticed the tufts of fur around the body.

"Yeah. Regardless of what it is, if it's a match to the fur at last night's scene, it's going to be helpful."

"There's going to be hell to pay. And that's insane," the chief told me.

"But if I'm right, there won't be any more Goatman murders."

I really was taking my career into my hands with that statement. Strat wouldn't fire me if I was wrong, but my credibility would go way, way down.

But I wasn't wrong.

I wondered how I hadn't seen it before. Everything in this case was about fury. The Native Americans getting the short end of the stick in 1666 — and the first report of Goatman that same year. Slavery. Pendleton Cartier during the Civil War. The Cartiers moving away. It'd take some research, but that was all going to tie in. I'd even profiled the unsub as a rage-based killer.

Then Mr. Hawkins's uncle, furious about segregation. Even the original Goatman legend about the man whose goat herd was harmed seeking revenge. Mission-based killings of Carter III and Farnsworth, complete with decapitation, hoofprints at the latter scene, and a burning cross as a giant "hey, stupid" in case we couldn't put it together. Vee's main characteristic was anger.

Jeremiah had lured him out by screeching. It was a straight-up challenge. His great-uncle told him to screech like that in the woods if he ever needed help. Uncle Josh had been a Goatman. He'd've talked to Jeremiah about discipline, and Jeremiah straight-up told me he joined the Marines to avoid becoming a Goatman. Overcome anger rather than be overcome by it. It was why Father Kelly's source had meditated on Ignatius of Loyola's *Spiritual Exercises*.

Now we just needed to find the "dark magics" part. Preferably before Randolph Johnson Cartier IV sued us for shooting his son. Who'd killed his father.

While in Goatman form.

Goatman had been much bigger. I suppose he'd gone back to normal size when he died. So, what about his wounds?

"Chief? Please ask the ME to check whether the wound tracks are less than 5.56 and nine-millimeter. If there are bullets still in him, and the entry channel is smaller than those bullets…"

"Then he changed back from Goatman to Vee." Brown shook his head. "That's ridiculous. I'm not asking the ME that."

"He'll have dropped the axe between here and Glenn Dale Hospital," I pointed out. "It'll have DNA on it."

"This is definitely the stupidest conversation I've ever had as a police officer."

"Mission-based. We already know the motive wasn't sex. Could be drugs—he was a user. But it's more likely it's one or more perceived injustices."

"I'll arrange for an immediate autopsy," the chief told me. "And depending on the results, I might be charging you."

I thought about bringing up *In re Neagle*—I *had* been defending US military personnel—but decided not to burn that bridge. The BAU was here by invitation.

On the solemn drive back to the station, though, I did place three phone calls.

Chapter Nine

Since I needed to sit down for a while, and we were all going to end up in the conference room anyway, I went directly there. I'll grant there was a bit of showmanship involved. I still had a lot of reading to do, but I wasn't supposed to because of the concussion. I downloaded an ebook and had the software read it to me. However, the real show happened a few hours later, after word got around that the ME was driving his results over.

Dutch Yost, Omar Crosby, Winters, and LeClair had already joined me in the conference room. The door opened, and Chief Brown walked in.

We'd no more than sat back down when the door opened again and two men entered.

The first one was tall, blond, and angular. He wore a nice suit.

"Chief? Special Agent-In-Charge Thomas Stratton, FBI Behavioral Analysis Unit. This is Captain Michael Creswell, United States Marine Corps. We came up from Quantico."

They shook hands all around, and then Strat reached into his jacket.

"Gun," he said. And handed me a Glock.

I checked it, chambered a round, and holstered it. Just about everyone else frowned.

But the chief just looked at the ME, who took it as a signal to begin. He was a small man with white hair, and he wore a clean lab coat over his dress shirt, slacks, and bow tie.

"The decedent, Randolph Johnson Cartier V, died of incised wounds that severed his carotid artery. The thirty-one bullet wounds probably would have killed him anyway." The ME peered at us over his rimless half-glasses. "Two items of interest. Most of the bullet wound tracks are at a rising angle, as if the shooters were shorter. I'm not sure why they were basically sitting on the ground, but that's about the right height. And the wound channels are too small."

He held up a hand. "Don't start with the Goatman stories. I've already heard 'em. I'm telling you I've got a nine-mil lodged next to the heart at the end of a channel nowhere near nine millimeters wide. I've got a 5.56 intact, in his brain, that went through a smaller hole in the skull. I stuck a plastic rod in his head. The 5.56 one didn't fit. I can't explain why the wound tracks closed up like this. Most of them aren't as deep as they should be, either. Frequently there are surprises with ballistic injuries. But not like this.

"I also can't explain how he made it as far as he did with thirty-one bullets in him. Sure, adrenaline surge." The ME shook his head. "He should have bled out a lot faster."

"How close was the shooter?" Chief Brown asked.

"Pointblank range. There's stippling around the entry wounds."

"So, they should have recognized he was a kid," the chief stated.

"The evidence doesn't tell me that," the ME countered. "The decedent made no effort to flee or get out of the line of fire. Entry angles are roughly similar for all thirty-one shots: to the front and angled upward. No bullet wounds to the back or from the side. He did not duck or run or successfully back up."

"He could have been lying on the ground with them looming over him," Winters offered.

"No," Dutch Yost stated. "If he were on the ground, any misses would be in the ground. We haven't found a bullet from a single miss. They're way to hell and gone in the woods."

The back-and-forth continued for some time.

Strat waited until the conversation had veered way down in the weeds, then asked his question.

"What happened when you called the phone number on the second Goatman's card?"

"It's not a Goatman!" Chief Brown insisted.

Strat held up a hand. "Someone handed Agent Watson a card. It says Goatman on it, and there's a phone number. What happened when you called it?"

"Voicemail." I could hear the disgust in LeClair's voice.

Strat and Yost both laughed. Then Strat pulled out his own phone and punched in the numbers. He put it on speaker.

Someone picked up. "Goatman."

"Goatman?" Strat repeated.

"Yes."

Strat and Chief Brown exchanged glances.

"What's a Goatman?"

"Body of a man, head and hooves of a goat. I assume you are law enforcement personnel calling from the Bowie, Maryland area."

"Quite right. My apologies. I'm Special Agent-In-Charge Thomas Stratton from the FBI. I'm here with the Bowie police chief, the ME, Detectives LeClair and Winters, Officers Crosby and Yost, Special Agent Tiffany Watson, and Captain Michael Creswell, Marine Corps."

The line was silent for just a minute. Then the voice asked, "BAU?"

"Yes."

"Captain Creswell, I assume you are Jeremiah Hawkins' commanding officer?"

Creswell didn't twitch, didn't blink. His "yes" was uninflected. But I got the idea that he was surprised at that question.

"Good man," the voice continued. "I do hope no one is under arrest."

"Not yet," Chief Brown answered.

I gave him points for a straight answer.

"Good. Special Agent Watson, are you the agent I handed my card to last night?"

"Yes, I am."

"Oh, good. And are Jeremiah and Father Kelly okay?"

"Father Kelly is fine. Jeremiah and I got thrown around a bit," I answered.

"But you fought off Vee. Mortally wounded him, if I'm not mistaken."

"Are you the one who finished him off with a blade?" Brown asked.

"Claws," the voice corrected. "I had to stop him before he reached 193. Plus, he did kill his grandfather and his distant cousin."

I felt eyes on me. Both Strat and Dutch Yost were looking my way, so I asked the question.

"Do you mean that Reynard Farnsworth is related to the Cartiers?"

"Yes. Look back at the generation that returned to Maryland in the 1900s."

"I've seen a couple references to that in the reading you left us."

"Oh, very good, Agent Watson! I was hoping you'd pick up on that."

I took a breath and a risk. "You staged the library."

"Yes. I felt it was preferable to the burning cross he left over the body. If you check the pond, you should find the half-burned timbers. I moved the body because I wanted to change the staging, and I didn't want the killer to change it back."

"May I interrupt?" I asked.

"Of course."

"Where did you find the burning cross the first night?"

The caller gave us an address.

"You're having no trouble explaining this to us. Last night, you handed me a card. I think it was because you couldn't speak. You were all communicating with those screeches."

The voice laughed softly. "Very true, very true. We cannot talk while in goat form."

Strat pointed a finger at me and dipped his head in acknowledgment.

"Pardon me if I use a bad word here," I continued. "So, you *are* weregoats?"

"Apology accepted." He sounded amused. "As long as you remember it has nothing to do with the full moon."

"I know. It's anger, isn't it?" I asked.

"Yes. Yes, it is."

"How does that work?" Strat asked. "Lots of people are angry, but they apparently only turn into Goatmen in Bowie."

"An excellent point. We don't know, not for sure."

I spoke up. "The roleplaying book said 'fury and dark magics.' It's both, isn't it? Not just anger, but an intense, burning rage about something you can't do anything about. The unfair treaty with the Native Americans, slavery, Pendleton Cartier losing his son in the Civil War, segregation..."

"Very good. That's our best understanding. As far as the dark magics, we do not know what was involved, and we certainly would not want to recreate whatever was done. There does seem to be a geographic locus. Before you ask, no, we don't understand why one person is affected and not another."

"You keep saying 'we,'" Strat noted. "You know about the Behavioral Analysis Unit. You've read the memoirs. So, you know that sometimes 'we' tells us we're dealing with a single individual."

"Hance in the Forces of Evil murders, yes." Goatman tossed the relevant case right back at Strat. "But I assure you, 'we' is the correct pronoun."

"How many of you are there?" Strat asked.

I saw Winters shaking his head. I think in his mind we were playing into the speaker's Goatman fantasy. My aching shoulder begged to differ.

"Ah, that is the question, is it not?" the voice parried. "It would be... unwise... to name names. Perhaps not all of you believe me, and this is the sort of case where information gets out despite best efforts."

"This really is a curse for you, isn't it?" I asked.

"I have come to think of it as a psychological and physiological condition," the voice said. "Most of us have developed ways of coping with it. However practiced we may be, we suspect that much of the public would not be comfortable with us living openly among them. Or even living openly apart from them."

"That logically follows if I grant your first premise," Strat responded.

My boss was trying really hard.

"That we Goatmen exist?"

"How do we know you didn't kill Cartier and Farnsworth?" The chief's blunt question came without warning.

The other end of the line went silent. "I suppose you do not know," the voice admitted. "One moment, please."

Goatman put us on hold.

After closer to two minutes, he came back on.

"My apologies. We have agreed to show you what we know. To show *some* of you *some* of what we know, I should say. Agent Watson, Jeremiah Hawkins, Father Kelly... and Officer Yost. You may bring any weapons you wish."

A number of people spoke at once. Chief Brown and Winters objected. Captain Creswell said he wasn't sending his Marine into a trap. I sat back and waited.

"Fine," the voice said. "Captain, you may come, too." He paused. "Obviously, we are compromising our safe house, and it will tell you a lot about us. We ask that you not take anything with you. If you wish to photograph or take notes, that is fine with us. We ask that you not leave any audio- or video-monitoring devices."

"Why me?" Dutch Yost asked.

"A few reasons, officer. First, you have a hex sign on your house."

"I grew up in southeastern Pennsylvania. That doesn't mean I think signs have any power."

"No, but we can read the signs, and yours includes the symbols for faith, hope, and love.

"Second, we need a liaison. It is possible you will never hear from us again, but we would like two of you to be local residents. Should we ever need to meet, you and Father Kelly could find your way back to the safe house. We anticipate that Jeremiah Hawkins will be stationed elsewhere and that Agent Watson may be working on a case outside the area.

"Third, each of you have particular skills and knowledge, and we are simply curious to see what you will conclude. Thank you for your call."

Goatman hung up.

Strat recovered his phone from the middle of the table and called the FBI. After a short conversation, he reported, "Voice over internet protocol, and he's using a VPN."

"He already had that set up when he handed me his card," I said. "Goatman is tech-savvy."

"This *perp* is tech-savvy," Winters corrected. "And he's inviting you to step into a trap."

"He's definitely speaking for a group," Strat stated. "He's intelligent. Middle-aged or a little more. He's formal without overdoing it, and he never used a contraction, so he's likely well-off and well-educated. A police officer, an agent, two Marines, and a priest... I think he genuinely believes he's allowing the strongest team possible without being gauche. It would violate his code of honor to ambush you. By all means, have a response team ready, of course."

We discussed it for a while, but in the end, that's what we did.

CHAPTER TEN

Strat took a hotel room down the hall from me. At 7:10 the next morning, he knocked on my door. I was already up and dressed.

"He called at seven o'clock sharp," Strat reported. "I wrote down directions and landmarks."

We looked up the road on Google Maps. It was halfway between Bowie and the Beltsville Agricultural Research Center.

"How are you with going in there?" Strat asked.

"I'll be careful, Strat, but you were right yesterday. It's not an ambush. He's Goatman #2. I realized you're right about the age, too. The white-streaked fur? He's older."

Strat didn't say anything about that. He hadn't come to terms with Goatman being real. I showed him the breakfast place in Bowie Town Center, and we walked into police headquarters at eight o'clock sharp. Jeremiah Hawkins, Captain Creswell, Father Kelly, and Dutch Yost were already waiting.

"Dutch, you shouldn't go in there alone," Omar Crosby said.

"We've got two law enforcement, two Marines, and a priest. He's giving up a location. The least we can do is see what he wants."

"The least we can do is catch him."

"I thought about it last night, and we could probably charge him with a single count of interfering with an investigation."

Chief Brown came out of his office. "The Cartiers are suing the city, the police force, and the FBI. Everybody's upset about the racial incident and worried about when he's going to strike again. We need to seriously consider going into this place in force."

"There's time to do that later." Strat's tone was polite, but he wasn't wasting any words. "He thinks he has a deal, and he's more likely to give you more if you go along with it."

"What if it's a trap?"

"Then sending five people in instead of everyone is still a better idea."

Like I said, Strat wasn't wasting any words this morning. But he wasn't arguing against sending me nor was he trying to take my place, so he really didn't think it was a trap. I suspected that was just killing him inside, but he wasn't going to do anything to undermine me in front of the local force.

By nine o'clock, the locals had a plan. We moved out. I was under no illusion that Strat and I would have any influence. If the chief decided SWAT should move in, he'd give the order. In fact, I expected he would.

And they'd come up empty. Goatman #2 didn't call Strat back without thinking things through. My read was that the Goatmen were long gone from wherever we were headed. But, yeah, I can see why Chief Brown would want the SWAT team there—just in case we were right about having put thirty-one rounds in Goatman #1 and not quite killing him.

I pulled off 197 onto a gravel road, driving Strat's SUV. Mine was still being processed. Dutch Yost rode shotgun. The others were in the back seat. Officer Yost climbed out when we reached a fence.

It was unlocked and swung open easily, as Goatman #2 had told Strat it would. As we continued on, I congratulated myself for insisting on the FBI vehicle. Yost's patrol car would have struggled with this... I stopped myself before I referred to it as a goat trail.

There had been some erosion here. I dodged a washed-out section on the left and spared a glance at the sky. No clouds. Good. I didn't want to be back in here if it started raining. The trail skirted a small pond and then headed uphill.

"That's got to be the old tree in the directions." Yost pointed at a big old gnarled something-or-other. Oak? Trees aren't my thing.

There was sort of a place to pull over, so I did, and we got out.

"Fifty paces south," Yost read from Strat's notes.

"Seriously?" Captain Creswell asked.

He and Jeremiah both had M4s. I wasn't sure how. He could have brought them with him from Quantico. Or he could have contacts at any number of local bases.

"Wonder what Goatman's pace count is," Jeremiah said to no one in particular.

Yost pointed. "It's going to be that pile of man-made junk over there," he said.

We could see power lines in the distance, but the only man-made items right here were a couple empty drums and some pallets. We pulled those aside and found a storm cellar door set in the ground.

Yost produced gloves. "Put these on. Forensics will check for fingerprints and DNA. They'll find some. In six months or more, we'll probably find out these guys aren't in the system. But we get only one chance at this."

I nodded. Everything Yost said was spot-on.

The lock was open. Yost removed it and tested the door. It lifted a couple inches without a lot of effort.

Yost and I drew our service weapons. Well, I drew the replacement Strat had given me.

"I'd really prefer to have at least one of the M4s up front," Captain Creswell said.

"I don't think you'll need it," Father Kelly said.

"Alright," Yost announced. "Captain Creswell and I will go in first. Agent Watson, you and Jeremiah cover us."

I thought about arguing that Goatman #2 seemed to like Jeremiah, Father Kelly, and me. But I'd lose that fight. On the bright side, nobody here wanted to arrest me.

"We're going in," Yost spoke into the radio on his shoulder.

"Roger."

Jeremiah and I eased the doors all the way open. They were heavy but moved fairly easily. Yost and Creswell started down the stairs.

"Clear!"

I went down the stairs next, followed by Father Kelly. Jeremiah indicated he'd guard the entrance. Smart move.

The stairs were twice as wide as a regular staircase and shallow — each was only a couple inches high. They were built of rough-cut timbers and seemed to go on and on. Once I reached the room at the bottom, I understood.

It was a barn. The wooden floor still had the remains of straw here and there. A number of... I'm not a farm girl, so I don't know the right word. Pens? Stalls? Places for animals — or Goatmen.

The wooden walls were interrupted only by a small door on the far side of the room. The doorknob looked like it had been replaced. More than once, I think.

I nodded to Officer Yost and Captain Creswell. Yost flung the door open, and Creswell charged through. Yost and I were right behind him.

The corridor was low and narrow. It ended at another door. Yost flung that one open, too.

We charged into the 1970s. The walls here were knotty-pine paneling, the carpet was an orange-brown shag, and the lampshades had actual fringe. Bookcases were built right into the walls. Goatman had left the lights on for us.

Creswell motioned toward a doorless opening in the right-side wall. He eased up to the corner, and Yost went through. "Clear!" A few seconds later, I heard another "Clear!"

"Kitchen and pantry," Yost reported.

I eyed the two doors in the left wall. When I moved toward the first, Yost motioned he'd enter while Creswell stayed back to cover both doors with his rifle.

I opened the door. Yost went in, and I followed. It was a bunkroom. Three beds against the left wall and one in the middle of the right wall with room for another beyond that. The near end of the right wall had another door.

This was starting to feel like a D&D dungeon.

We went through the door and cleared a bathroom. There was another door....

I went back to the bunkroom. "Captain Creswell? We have a bunkroom and a bathroom. We're going to open a door in the bathroom, and I think it's the second door you're watching."

"Roger that."

Sure enough. That was it. This was basically an underground house. Or underground Goatman lair, I suppose. We ran a quick check to make sure we hadn't missed any doors or rooms.

Captain Creswell spoke up. "I'm not going to be of much use examining this place, so I'll send Hawkins down and take his spot."

"Thanks," I told him.

"I'm headed up, too," Yost said, "to radio so that no one sends in SWAT."

Father Kelly examined the main room with interest. He'd gone straight for the bookshelves. I joined him.

"Gaps," he said.

"There were books left in a Little Free Library at the first crime scene." I saw the books were organized by subject. "History. Quite a bit of theology."

"Interesting mix," Father Kelly commented. "Much of this is Protestant, but I see Loyola's *Spiritual Exercises* and Thomas à Kempis's *The Imitation of Christ*. Oh! John of the Cross's *Dark Night of the Soul*."

"I'm going to guess these belonged to your source in the 1970s, Father," I said. "I'm going to further guess that he didn't like being a Goatman."

"If it is anger-based, he was trying to control it."

"Yes."

Jeremiah and Officer Yost walked in.

"They were antsy, but no SWAT raid," Yost reported.

With the M4 pointed at the floor and his finger off the trigger, Jeremiah just turned in place, taking it all in. Finally, he whistled.

"This is something else. The '70s want their safe house back." Another turn. "Goatman comes in from whatever Goatmen do at night and crashes in the stable. In the morning—or however that works—he fits through the human-sized tunnel and hangs out here until he's pretty sure he won't Goatman-out again, right?"

The rest of us traded glances. "Makes sense to me," I said.

A few minutes later, Father Kelly found the first note.

"'Please return the books on this shelf to the Little Free Library at Northridge Park. If possible, please return the books found there to this shelf.'"

Dutch Yost laughed. "Your Goatman is an OCD librarian." He stepped closer to a set of shelves and stooped down to pluck a big flat book off the second shelf from the bottom. "Which makes this a clue."

The book had a note sticking out from between the pages.

"'Read this.' Real subtle there, pal." Yost examined the book. "This is a manuscript, not a printed book. *A History of the Curse*."

He began reading aloud.

"'In 1666, the colony of Maryland signed the Articles of Peace and Amity with a dozen tribes of...' The word Indians is crossed-out, and Native Americans is written above it in a different hand. 'The treaty was unjust, restricting their rights, but not those of the colonists. In particular, they were to throw down their arms if they met an Englishman in the woods.

"'A dissenting faction, perhaps no more than a handful of people, rejected the English, their religion, their weapons, and the advice of their own spiritual leaders. They invoked the Curse. How we do not know, for they also rejected writing, and if there was an oral tradition, it appears to have died out. This writer puts greater weight on a Jesuit's sighting that year of what may have been the first Goatman. An oral tradition that did survive states that at least some colonists whose deaths in the forests were attributed to wild animals were actually killed by a Goatman.'

Yost looked up. "The writer claims people turn into Goatmen only within an area roughly bound by Route 3/301 east, 214 south, Beltway and Parkway west, and 198 and 32 to the north. He spends a lot of words saying they don't know why it's localized and don't ever try to duplicate the curse. This is far too extensive to be a practical joke. Whoever wrote this believes what he is writing. He may be wrong. I mean, he must be. But he believes it."

"I agree," I said.

Yost resumed reading just the highlights. "'…we know little of subsequent Goatmen until the 1850s, when Hawkins, who was a slave, escaped from the Cartier plantation. He traveled north via the Underground Railroad but was caught somewhere in Pennsylvania and returned under the provisions of the Fugitive Slave Act of 1850.

"'Hawkins was furious and later recounted that it took four men to hold him. Pendleton Cartier was also furious and ordered him punished. Hawkins swore he'd kill any man who whipped him. Three weeks later, they found the overseer in the woods with his throat ripped out.'"

"Dang straight," Jeremiah said.

Neither law enforcement officer in the room chose to argue with that. Father Kelly managed a disapproving look.

"He's quoting Hawkins here. 'I felt forsaken. By the government. By mankind. By the Good Lord Himself. When I got mad enough, I changed. Each time they whipped me, I got madder. I would run off when I felt the change coming. There was a house that had burned and been abandoned, but the cellar was still there. I hid out below, stashed supplies. I'd be gone for days at a time sometimes, and Cartier would be powerful mad when I came back. For a while, I didn't know which of us was the madder, but he didn't change, so I guess I was.

"'Then one of his sons fell at Gettysburg. Cartier went mad. Not angry-mad. Crazy-mad. He ranted at the Union, made threats, busted up the furniture. His wife and younger children left, supposedly to recover at a distant relative's. And folk started dying.

"'There were wild animal attacks where there ain't been none in years, not since 'fore I was born. The new state constitution freed us in October 1864, too late in the year to head north. I said I would stay on for wages, and Cartier lost his mind. He struck me with a riding crop. I threw him against a tree and left.

"'That night, we both felt the Curse. I heard him screeching and tracked him. He was tracking me. We found each other and fought. All but kilt each other. He crawled away first. Cartier never faced me in public again.'"

"I never heard this part before," Jeremiah said.

"I think your Great Uncle Josh didn't want you to hear it," I offered.

Jeremiah thought a moment, then started slowly nodding his head. "Yeah. He was big on self-discipline. 'What other people make you do don't count, boy. You got to control yourself.' This puts a whole different take on it."

"That's for sure," Yost muttered.

Yost resumed reading aloud. "'Cartier sent the night riders after me. I tore 'em up. Shot me a couple o' times, but I shrugged it off… Cartier got killed, but it weren't me. He ambushed an Army patrol, and the Yankees can fight. Killed a couple of 'em, but their officer carried a brace of Colts, and he seen the elephant. Didn't stop for nothing until he emptied both revolvers into Cartier twice and then went at him with his sword. We heal good, but nobody heal *that* good."

"'The officer said he'd killed a wolf and didn't see why anyone should make a fuss about it. I never did figure out whether he knew about the Curse or not. The Cartiers left Maryland.'

"Whoever wrote this says there was another Goatman between Hawkins and his own mentor. And listen to this!

"'I have three in my care. No names, not even here, not until each passes on. Soldiers all, and that may have played a part. Coming home to something less than the ideal they fought for definitely figured in. I bought the property with the old cellar Hawkins used and fixed it up. We stay here when we feel the Curse coming on.

"'We have saved a place for another, not of our group. He has not mastered the Curse and has been seen. Tales are passed along in the community, and I do not know what to do.'"

Yost looked up. "Whether he just believes it's true or whether it really is, that is some heavy stuff to carry around."

Jeremiah nodded solemnly. "Great Uncle Josh was always really serious when he talked about Goatman. I don't know why he didn't tell me about this first Hawkins."

"Like you said, he was in the war. I assume your uncle was one of the three the writer mentored." Yost looked around. "This must be the old cellar, greatly enlarged. Do you suppose they did it themselves?"

"I suspect so," I said. "If a Goatman decided to dig, I imagine he could out-shovel a regular person. The dorm, the library, the spiritual disciplines, the mentorship—it all speaks to them turning inward and watching out for each other. This group aren't serial killers."

"You're missing something, Agent Watson," Yost said.

"What's that?"

"A whole generation of Goatmen."

"Yeah, you're right. Let's go with your theory that one of the three this author mentored was Jeremiah's Great Uncle Josh. Another of the three would be the man who came to confession, right, Father Kelly?"

"Yes," the priest said. "That seems likely to me. It explains why Jeremiah and I have each been so confident in our own candidate for Goatman. We were both right."

"And a third."

"And a fourth," Yost corrected. "The fourth is the one behind all the sightings."

"Or behind the early sightings," I said. "The three who fought in the war—that's World War II, right? So, they were probably born about 1920 to 1925."

"That makes sense," Jeremiah said. "The fourth who was seen would be young and dumb in 1957. So born about 1940. He could be all the sightings up to 2007."

"You're right," I said. "Of course, some of them could be the writer and the other three trying to keep him under control."

"He either stopped, was stopped, or got smarter about it," Yost put in. "So how do we get to Vee?"

"He's angry, he's already using drugs, he gets a bad drug interaction and loses it," I suggested. "You've seen cases like that, right?"

"Definitely."

I realized something. "Vee wasn't clueless. Jeremiah, he regarded your screeches as a challenge. He came to attack. He knew there were other Goatmen."

"Can't have been the writer, Uncle Josh, or Father Kelly's parishioner," Jeremiah said. "Probably not the third one, because he'd be a hundred years old. The young one from '57... would be about 80. Could have clued Vee in, I suppose."

"There's also Goatman #2," I said. "He seemed older."

Jeremiah winced. "I hope we didn't make him take out his protégé. That's all too Obi-wan."

"Yeah, I hear that," I said. "But he didn't seem 80, either. Not that I know a thing about how Goatmen are affected by age."

"This probably goes into some detail," Yost offered. "I think what I read is just the introduction. I'm still not sure I believe any of this. But for the sake of argument, a line of Goatmen from 1666 to now, some of whom we know. Three from the Greatest Generation, a Boomer, and then Vee and Number Two.

"Vee killed Randolph Johnson Cartier III and Reynard Farnsworth. Why?"

"What if the Cartiers left after Pendleton died to get away from the Curse?" Jeremiah asked. "Oh! What if they know the name Hawkins? I bet my name's been in the news the last couple of days."

"I will stay here and photograph the manuscript," Father Kelly said. "I can pray from here just as well."

The rest of us ran for the door.

Captain Creswell heard us pounding up the stairs. "What's the hurry?"

Yost thumbed his radio in response. "Chief, this is Yost. Do we have a unit on the initial suspect's house?"

"No, we don't," came the reply.

"Send one."

We piled into the FBI SUV, and I took the trail as quickly as I dared. Dutch Yost was still on his radio. I hit the lights and sirens when we reached 197. A couple patrol cars fell in behind us.

"Take Old Laurel-Bowie Road," Yost directed. He said something on the radio, and then I heard "Break" from someone else.

"Shots fired!" We all recognized the Hawkinses' address.

"Mile and a half," Yost told me.

That meant about a minute and a half because I was going to have to slow down to make turns. Ninety seconds is a long time when shots have been fired. Our fight with Goatman Vee might have lasted that long. Maybe.

I just missed a knucklehead who tried to merge from a side road. Somehow, he overlooked the SUV with lights and sirens. I almost took out a parked car dodging him.

Then I had two blocks before the road curved right and came to a T at the Lanham-Severn Road. I planned to take the corner as fast as I safely could. My seatbelt would lock up, but—

A sedan traveling as fast as we were flashed across the bridge.

"Gun!" Yost, Creswell, and Jeremiah all shouted it. Two rounds struck the windshield.

"Brace!"

I took my foot off the gas so that I hit the car just behind the rear wheels rather than in a classic T-bone.

If you've heard of a PIT maneuver—that's a precision immobilization technique or a pursuit intervention technique, depending on your department—this wasn't it. A PIT maneuver is supposed to make contact with the side of the other vehicle, and then the officer or agent swerves into the vehicle to cause it to spin out and hopefully stall. It is *not* ramming a fleeing vehicle at right angles at forty-five miles an hour.

My airbag deployed, as did Officer Yost's. That is not a pleasant experience, and I would have bruises on top of my previous bruises. I spun the wheel to the right and felt the SUV scrape along the guardrail on the west side of the road. We skidded to a stop.

Jeremiah hit the back of my seat, but he had his door open before my airbag finished deflating. So, we must have come off the guardrail at some point.

I'd heard three shots from the right rear. I looked across the remains of my airbag. The passenger riding shotgun in the other vehicle was dead. His weapon was pointing at us. All three of Creswell's rounds were headshots. Dang, that was some shooting.

The sedan's engine was still running, but the driver was busy wiping blood off his face. And freaking out.

"Back right!" Yost barked. He'd leveled his pistol without getting out of the SUV. "Roll down your window and put both hands out! Now!"

I swung my door open and stepped out. The passenger in the back right seat was complying.

"Open the door from the outside!"

Jeremiah had already circled around behind the sedan, M-4 at the ready. "Back left! Same thing! Roll your window down and reach both hands outside! Do it now, Dylan! I am not fooling around!"

I got around the front of the SUV as the back right passenger emerged. I cuffed him. By the time I was done, someone else was cuffing the back left passenger, and another officer was getting the driver out. He immediately fell to his knees and barfed all over the road.

Next thing I knew, Strat was there.

"Are you okay?" he asked.

"Yeah. I'm gonna need more painkillers."

Creswell came over. "Hell of a piece of driving, ma'am."

"Hell of a shot, all three."

"Dumbass had his finger on the trigger. Put two through your back right window while we were skidding. I know I'm not a cop, but sooner or later, he was going to hit someone."

"You did the right thing." I started to shake my head and thought better of it.

"Who are these guys?" he asked. "Reminded me of Iraq and Syria."

"Jeremiah?" I asked. "I heard you call one kid Dylan."

"Guys I used to run with. The one you cuffed is Jay. Ma'am, is my family okay?"

"They're fine," Strat answered. "These guys shot up the house, but nobody got hit. Watson, you lit out like you knew it was going to happen."

"That cellar's a safe house. Fully stocked, including a manuscript history of the Goatmen. There was a Hawkins back in the 1850s and '60s. Went up against another who was a Cartier."

Strat processed that in about two seconds. He turned and called, "Chief!"

"Somebody should go get Father Kelly. We left him in the safehouse taking pictures of the manuscript."

"Crosby went in," Strat said.

"Good. Thanks. Strat, there's going to be something, a burner call maybe, from somebody in the Cartier Group to one of the gang-bangers."

My boss nodded. "We'll get it. Or Bowie will. Any ideas who?"

"Could be RJ Four," I answered. "Doesn't feel right, though. Cecilia said he'd do something financial if he were angry." A thought struck me. "We suspect RJ the Third was meeting someone the night he was killed. Could be someone who'd know the family Goatman history. Whether you believe it or not, it's motive. Five kills Three and Farnsworth, then a Hawkins shot him up, and a second Goatman finished him."

"So, someone who knew the family history put out a hit on Hawkins. And uses his old gang to do it. That's someone who can get into records, knows their way around Bowie."

The Bowie chief arrived in time to hear part of that. "Interesting line of thought. I think you all get checked out by the paramedics, and I'll let you watch the interrogation. I'll have an officer take you home first, corporal."

"Thank you."

"And, captain, I'll let our outside agency go over the shoot, but the officer in the car behind you saw him shooting the SUV before and during the collision."

Chapter Eleven

Three guesses what the top story was that day.

The Lanham-Severn Road was closed for hours. Anyone who wanted to get across the railroad tracks had to divert east to 197 or west to 193. That plus the shot-up FBI vehicle pretty much guaranteed everyone in Bowie knew about it.

LeClair and Winters handled the interrogations. LeClair did a masterful job and got Jay to give up a name. Sheila.

"I ain't s'pposta know, but I heard someone in the background call her that once."

In the viewing room, I wrote down thoughts and held my notebook out to Strat.

Sheila. Maybe the COO of the Cartier Group? If so, she'll be blonde, young for that position, upper-class, and have been having an affair with RJ III. That's why the third marriage with Miranda Summersby has lasted longer than the others. It wasn't his primary relationship. Revenge for killing her lover, plus she knows the Cartier family secret. I'm guessing RJ III never told his kids, and that's why Vee killed him — for not preparing him.

Strat raised an eyebrow, then penned: *It holds together. Let's check it out.*

It didn't take very long to find the Cartier Group website. And there she was: Sheila Abercrombie, chief operations officer for the last eight years. Blonde. Not even forty, and already a COO.

Chief Brown pulled LeClair and Winters to give them the information. LeClair slowly switched his line of questioning to previous jobs Jay and the others had handled for Sheila. Before long, Bowie PD was working on warrants.

By then, Crosby and Father Kelly had come in from the safe house.

"Goes against the grain," Omar Crosby said, "but we left it just like we found it. Father Kelly has pictures, and we didn't consciously bring anything out with us except that shelf of books marked for the Little Free Library. Locard's Exchange Principle, though—we'll have tracked something in and out if nothing else."

"Well, a deal's a deal, and we didn't have probable cause or exigent circumstances," Chief Brown said. "Found probable cause for everything else, though. I still don't think there's an actual Goatman out there, but whoever this guy is, he's been helpful. Of course, I'm not ruling out that he killed Vee."

Well, yeah. He had.

"The rest of this is going to take time. Bowie's on edge. Remember, there was a burning cross. There's a vigil tonight, and they're going to march from the university to the racetrack. It's a mile and a quarter. Here's what I want to do..."

The chief had called in some favors. Fire trucks and public works trucks blocked the side roads at intersections. Bowie PD, Prince George's PD, the Prince George's Sheriff's Department patrol cars, and an FBI SUV escorted the march.

The students were motivated and had erected a stage during the day. People from Bowie were driving up Race Track Road from the other direction. Officers were directing them into makeshift parking areas.

We stood off to one side as the speeches began. They showed genuine concern, fear, and some rabblerousing. Not as much as I expected, though. And the students held each other to time limits fairly well.

Chief Brown let things go on until he got a radio call.

"Baker Four, 10-15 at the address the chief gave us."

"Roger, Baker Four," the chief said. "Great job. Call my cell."

Good move. The chief needed details, and they didn't need to go out on the air. After the phone call, he brought the rest of us up to speed.

"First, when we sent that email to Sheila Abercrombie's Cartier Group address claiming to be Jay demanding help, she went straight to that property owned by the Cartier Group. Proof of a male and a female inside. Looks like it was being used to rendezvous. Good chance of DNA. Blood outside, fragments of charred wood, fur, and eyeglasses matching Randolph Johnson Cartier III's prescription. Chip in the sidewalk consistent with an axe. DNA is going to take weeks or months, of course."

Strat nodded. "Always."

"They found a burner there. We'll need time to work with the carrier. But it called Jay's phone."

We conferred, and then Chief Brown approached the stage.

"Could I get a word after this speaker is done, please?"

The two students who guarded the stairs up to the platform gave him considering looks.

"What are you planning to say? Are you going to tell us to calm down?"

"I'm going to announce an arrest in the murders, as of about ten minutes ago."

Those were the magic words. The speaker wound down, and the chief motioned us to follow him.

"Next, Chief Brown has asked to speak."

There was scattered applause and some boos.

"I know there has been a lot of speculation about recent cases. I want you to know that they are all related: the man found dead in Northridge Park, the man found dead here, the young man on the WB&A Trail, and the young man shot in the traffic collision this morning."

He waited for the buzz in the crowd to settle.

"I'd like to thank the Prince George's County Police, the FBI's Behavioral Analysis Unit, and the United States Marine Corps."

We filed up onto the stage. The PG chief. Strat, and I. Captain Creswell and Corporal Hawkins, both in dress uniforms.

"This case goes back to events in the 1850s and '60s. It was very much racially motivated *then*. This week, two men — Raymond Johnson Cartier III and Reynard Farnsworth — were murdered, and burning crosses were set up near the bodies." He held up a hand. "I know you didn't hear that detail about the first one. A third party put it out and moved the body. We have conferred with the state's attorney, and evidence will be presented to a grand jury that the perpetrator of those two murders is now dead.

"Corporal Jeremiah Hawkins was arrested on suspicion of murder. Frankly, that was a poor decision on our part, and I want to publicly apologize."

Jeremiah came forward. "Thank you." They shook hands.

"Corporal Hawkins and Special Agent Tiffany Watson combined his family history and her profile and were able to locate Raymond Johnson Cartier V. He promptly attacked them and was mortally wounded in the struggle. Had he survived, I would be charging him with the murder of his grandfather and Mr. Farnsworth.

"This morning, we acquired additional information suggesting that Corporal Hawkins might be targeted. His family home was shot up in a drive-by, but no one was hit. The getaway car fired on an FBI vehicle. One of the gunmen was killed in an exchange of fire, and the other three are in custody.

"Within the last hour, we have arrested Sheila Abercrombie of the Cartier Group for contracting the attempted hit on the Hawkins family."

Again, he waited for the crowd to settle.

"Our forensics team is working overtime, but real life isn't like television. It's going to be months before we're able to confirm or disprove any number of things. To the best of our knowledge, we have arrested and charged all surviving suspects."

A shout came from the crowd.

"Was Goatman involved?"

There were a few laughs and some mutters of disapproval. The chief waited it out again.

"No comment."

AUTHOR'S NOTE

All locations in and around Bowie are real, with the exception of the underground safe house. I have taken the liberty of creating the Hawkins and the Cartiers and assigning certain events and locations to them that historically belong to others.

ABOUT THE AUTHOR

Bjorn Hasseler is currently an academic success coach. He has held a number of jobs related to education, including military reenactor, library page, sports information director, assistant athletic director, and college adjunct instructor.

He began writing the summer after seventh grade when a teacher convinced the school district to let him take an Apple IIe home for the summer. Over the next several years, he attempted to cram all of the plots into one multi-generational universe.

Bjorn went to the library looking for the third book in Timothy Zahn's Thrawn Trilogy and found David Weber's Honor Harrington series. This led him to Eric Flint's 1632 universe.

He has written four novels and twenty-five short stories in the 1632/Ring of Fire alternate history universe. He unsuspectingly answered a request for help and ended up as the assistant editor of that universe's e-magazine, the Grantville Gazette. He is now editor-in-chief of its successor e-magazine, Eric Flint's 1632 & Beyond.

Bjorn lives near Laurel, Maryland. Once he's sure he hasn't enrolled students in the Fall, 1636 semester, he enjoys reading, theology, and gaming.

artist's rendition of Goatman

GOATMAN

ORIGINS: The earliest sighting of Goatmen is recorded in 520 BC, with the satyrs of Greek myth, cited as both lusty and violent creatures. Modern accounts of this cryptid, in one version or another, are reported from multiple regions in the US, including Texas, Pennsylvania, Louisiana, Florida, Michigan, Arkansas, Alabama, California, Kentucky, Indiana, and Maryland.

Lore presents two possible origin stories for the Maryland variant of this cryptid, with some details echoed in other regions. Some say it began with a goatherder driven crazy with rage when local teenagers killed his flock.

Others believe Goatman began as a scientist from the Beltsville Agricultural Research Center who experimented on goats. Something went wrong, turning him into a completely insane half-man, half-goat who reportedly wanders the area at night attacking cars with an axe.

DESCRIPTION: Said to be between six to eight feet tall, this cryptid has been described either as a hairy humanoid with the face of a man, or a man with the horns, legs, and hooves of a goat. The eyes are said to be red and the body powerful, but deformed.

Goatman is also known for being angry, aggressive, and blood-thirsty, making a high-pitched shrieking sound, and a having a pungent odor. He is said to posses the strength of two grown men and wield an axe. They are noted for being territorial.

This cryptid is said to live under bridges and in caves in more rural areas

LIFE CYCLE: Unknown

HISTORY: While there have been stories of some type of Goatman for a very long time, and from different regions, the accounts bear much similarity.

In some, Goatman is said to roam the night, attacking those parked in out-of-the-way places making out, luring away the male and killing him brutally with his axe, and then hanging him above the car to torment the female hiding within.

In other tales of the Goatman, he is said to mutilate local livestock and kill small animals, particularly dogs, beheading them or cleaving them in half. Often the body is never found.

There have been many sightings throughout the years, mostly of Goatman disappearing into wooded areas, and in some accounts of attacks on animals, there have been distinctively hooved footprints found near the remains.

Variations: Grunch, Waterford Sheepman, Pope Lick Monster, Proctor Valley Monster, Lake Worth Monster, Satyr, Faun, Krampus

Although Jason Whitley has worn many creative hats, he is at heart a traditional illustrator and painter. With author James Chambers, Jason collaborates and illustrates the sometimes-prose, sometimes graphic novel, *The Midnight Hour*, which is being collected into one volume by eSpec Books. His and Scott Eckelaert's newspaper comic strip, Sea Urchins, has been collected into four volumes. Along with eSpec Books' Systema Paradoxa series, Jason is working on a crime noir graphic novel. His portrait of Charlotte Hawkins Brown is on display in the Charlotte Hawkins Brown Museum.

CAPTURE THE CRYPTIDS!

Cryptid Crate is a monthly subscription box filled with various cryptozoology and paranormal themed items to wear, display and collect. Expect a carefully curated box filled with creeptastic pieces from indie makers and artisans pertaining to bigfoot, sasquatch, UFOs, ghosts, and other cryptid and mysterious creatures (apparel, decor, media, etc).

http://CryptidCrate.com